Ferdinand von Schirach w and has worked as a defen He published his first boo since published various sl and plays. Ferdinand von S translated into more than sold millions of copies worldwide. He lives in Berlin.

Katharina Hall is a freelance German to English translator who specialises in literary and academic texts. She is the editor of *Crime Fiction in German: Der Krimi* and runs the international crime blog 'Mrs. Peabody Investigates'. She lives in Wales.

Praise for Ferdinand von Schirach

'Rumpole by way of Rilke . . . one quickly develops a taste for von Schirach's unpredictable musings, a taste which becomes a full-blown addiction by the end of the book'   *Daily Telegraph*

'An exceptional prose stylist'   *New York Times*

'Meticulously crafted, pithy and mordantly amusing'
                                          Irish Times

'A magnificent storyteller'   *Der Spiegel*

Coffee and Cigarettes

Ferdinand von Schirach

Translated by Katharina Hall

BASKERVILLE
An imprint of JOHN MURRAY

First published as *Kaffee und Zigaretten* in German
in 2019 by Luchterhand Literaturverlag

First published in Great Britain in 2023 by Baskerville
An imprint of John Murray (Publishers)

This paperback edition published in 2024

1

A CIP catalogue record for this title is available from the British Library

Paperback ISBN 9781529345735
ebook ISBN 9781529345742

Typeset in Sabon by Hewer Text UK Ltd, Edinburgh

Printed and bound in Great Britain by Clays Ltd, Elcograf S.p.A.

John Murray policy is to use papers that are natural, renewable and recyclable products and
made from wood grown in sustainable forests. The logging and manufacturing processes are
expected to conform to the environmental regulations of the country of origin.

Carmelite House
50 Victoria Embankment
London EC4Y 0DZ

www.johnmurraypress.co.uk

John Murray Press, part of Hodder & Stoughton Limited
An Hachette UK company

The woods are lovely, dark and deep,
But I have promises to keep,
And miles to go before I sleep,
And miles to go before I sleep.

Robert Frost, 'Stopping by Woods on a Snowy Evening'

In the summer, he's down at the pond every day. He sits on the Chinese bridge leading to the small island, water lilies and marsh irises beneath him, catching occasional glimpses of carp, bream and tench. Dragonflies with huge compound eyes hover in the air before him. The gun dogs snap at them, but always miss. Dragonflies can do magic, his father says, but such tiny wonders that they're invisible to the human eye. It's only behind the old chestnut trees and the stone walls of the park that the other world begins. His isn't a happy childhood, things are too complicated, but later he'll always remember the slowness of those days.

His family never goes away on holiday. The high points of the year are Christmas, with its long Advent season, fox hunting with horses and hounds in the summer, and the big drive hunts of autumn, when the beaters eat stew, and drink beer and herbal schnapps in the hunting lodge courtyard.

Sometimes relatives come to stay. One aunt smells of lily of the valley, another of sweat and lavender. Their old fingers stroke his hair, and he has to bow and kiss their hands. He doesn't like it when they touch him, and he doesn't want to be around when they have their little chats.

Shortly before his tenth birthday, he's sent to a Jesuit boarding school. It lies in a dark, narrow Black Forest valley where winter reigns six months of the year, far from the nearest large town. The chauffeur drives him away from his home, away from the chinoiseries, the painted silk wallpaper and the curtains with the brightly coloured parrots. They drive through villages and empty landscapes, past lakes, and then down and ever deeper into the Black Forest. When they arrive, he's intimidated by the cathedral's huge dome, the baroque buildings and the priests' black soutanes. His bed is in a dormitory along with thirty other beds, and in the bathroom the washbasins are lined up next to one another on the wall. There's only cold water.

The first night he thinks: any minute, someone will turn on the lights again and say, 'How brave you were, it's all over now, you can go back home.'

He gets used to boarding school, the way that children get used to almost anything. But he feels like he doesn't belong, like something's missing that he can't articulate. The green and dark green of his former world gradually disappear, the colours in his head change. He doesn't yet know that his brain is linking perceptions 'falsely' with one another. He sees letters and smells and people as colours. He assumes that other children see the same things, only learning of the term *synaesthesia* much later on. One day, he shows the poems he's written about these colours to the priest who teaches German. The old man phones his mother – the boy is 'in peril', he says. Nothing more comes of it. When he gets the poems back, just the spelling mistakes are marked up in red.

His father dies when he is fifteen. He hadn't seen him in a number of years; his parents separated when he was young. His father had sent him postcards at boarding school – street scenes from Lugano, Paris and Lisbon. One time, there was a postcard from

Manila. It showed a man in a pale linen suit standing in front of the white Malacañan Palace. He imagines that his father looks just like this man.

The headmaster gives him money for the train ticket home. He doesn't take a suitcase because he can't think what to pack. All he has with him is a book. The bookmark between its pages is the post-card from Manila. On the journey, he tries to memo-rise every train station, every tree outside the window, every person in his compartment. He's convinced that everything will fragment if he can't remember it all.

He goes to the funeral on his own. A family chauf-feur drops him off in front of the chapel in Munich. He hears speeches about an odd stranger – about his excessive alcohol consumption, his charms and his fail-ings. He's never met the new wife sitting in the front row. She's wearing long black lace gloves, and all he can see beneath the veil is her red lipstick. There's a large photograph next to the coffin, but the man in it looks nothing like his father. An uncle, whom he's only ever seen twice, embraces him, kisses him on the forehead and tells him that he's 'blessed'. He feels uncomfortable, but smiles and responds politely. Later, on the cemetery path, the sun reflects on the coffin's polished wood. The earth he throws into the grave is wet from the previous night's rain. It sticks to his hand and he doesn't have a handkerchief to wipe it off.

A few weeks later, the autumn holidays begin. He sits by the fireplace in the entrance hall of the house. At his feet lie two dogs called Shakespeare and Whisky. Suddenly, every sound he hears is equally loud: the distant voices of his grandmother and the house-keeper, the tyres of the car the chauffeur is turning in front of the house, the shriek of a jay, the ticking of the grandfather clock. And now he sees everything in hyperreal detail – the oily shimmer in his teacup, the texture of the light green sofa, the motes of dust in the sunlight. He gets frightened. For a number of minutes, he can't move.

Once his breathing is calm again, he goes up to the library in search of some lines he once read. On 20 November 1811, Heinrich von Kleist and his close friend Henriette Vogel, who was suffering from cancer, journeyed to Kleiner Wannsee near Berlin. Both wished to die. They took rooms at a modest inn and composed farewell letters into the early hours of the morning. A letter from Kleist to his half-sister closes with the inscription 'Stimming's, near Potsdam, on the morning of my death'. On the afternoon of the following day, they ordered coffee and had chairs brought outside. Kleist shot Vogel in the chest and himself in the mouth, knowing that the temple was too risky. Shortly beforehand, he had written that he was 'contented and serene'.

The boy waits until everyone else has gone to bed, then heads to the bar, settles himself in an armchair and, taking small sips, works his way methodically through a bottle and a half of whisky. When he tries to get up, he stumbles and pulls over a small table, tipping the crystal decanters onto the floor. He watches blankly as the dark stain spreads. Down in the cellar, he opens the weapons cabinet, removes one of the shotguns and exits the house, leaving the door wide open. He walks to the elm tree that his father planted to mark his birth, sits on the ground and leans his back against the smooth trunk. From here, in the morning light, he sees the old house with its flight of steps and its white columns. The rondelle lawn is freshly mown; it smells of grass and rain. His father once told him that he'd placed an African gold coin under the elm tree, and said it would bring him luck. He puts the black barrel of the gun in his mouth.

It feels strangely cold on his tongue. Then he pulls the trigger.

The next morning, the gardeners find him lying in his own vomit, the shotgun in his arms. He was so drunk that he'd forgotten to load the cartridge. He tells no one about that night, in which he saw himself.

At the age of eighteen, he goes on holiday for the first time with his girlfriend. He'd worked for four weeks on a factory assembly line and his earnings are enough for the trip. They fly to Crete and travel for three hours across the mountains in an old bus, along ever narrower serpentine roads, then onwards to the southernmost tip of the island. They rent a room in a guesthouse – whitewashed wooden floors, white bedsheets. Beneath the window lies the Libyan Sea. The village has just a handful of houses and a tiny supermarket selling fruit, cheese, vegetables and bread. The owner bakes sweet biscuits and savoury pastries on alternate days, and that's what they live on. They spend their days at the beach. It's quiet.

At some point she wants to know why he is the way he is. How can a sunny person understand darkness? He thinks. He tries to explain using medical terms.

She listens and nods. Depression isn't a form of sadness, he says, it's something quite different. He knows that she won't understand.

In their room, she hangs her dress over the back of the chair. She stands in the bathroom, her slender body in front of the steamed-up mirror. He lies on the bed and watches her. The air is humid and warm. The world around him vanishes without resistance: it no longer has any sharp edges, the colours fade, noises disappear. The door to the bathroom closes, he's alone. Oil begins to drip from the ceiling onto his forehead, runs in streaks down the whitewashed walls, covers the wooden floor, the bed, the sheets, until everything is smooth and loses its shape. The room fills completely, the oil sloshes onto his face, into his ears and his mouth, clogging his eyes. He breathes it in, becomes numb, and then he himself is the blue-black oil.

Later, they lie sweaty and exhausted on the bed. After she falls asleep, he looks at her. He kisses her breasts, pulls the sheet up over her and sits on the balcony. The sea is black and alien. He can't remember whether he really told her all that stuff. And then he realises he has another sixty years of this ahead of him.

2

Fifty-four years ago, on the day of my birth, the League of Arab States imposed an import boycott on Burberry, the English raincoat manufacturer. The reason given was that the company did business with Israel. Back then, the League was boycotting several firms that had Lord Mancroft on their management boards. He was Jewish.

In London, they took a relaxed view. A spokesman for the company said it rarely rained in Arab countries anyway, and that 'laughably few' raincoats had been exported there to date.

3

In 1981, I spent the summer holidays in England. I was seventeen and meant to be improving my English. The man I stayed with in Yorkshire was impoverished landed gentry, whose only comment on the Queen was that she was 'very middle class'. He drove a thirty-year-old Rolls Royce and lived in a dilapidated fourteenth-century manor house. The roof of one wing was missing, the only heated area was the kitchen, and his most precious possessions were two slender Holland & Holland shotguns. The bedspread in my room smelled as though Oliver Cromwell had once slept in it, which was not entirely improbable. But I liked the stone house and its garden, the ancestral portraits blackened with age, and the moss on the windowsills. The bathtub was made of copper, and was so enormous that it took half an hour to fill. It had a dark, mahogany frame, and I remember how pleasant it was to lie there and read.

My host had idiosyncratic pedagogical ideas. His educational programme consisted of playing old David Niven films, reciting Kipling poems and otherwise leaving me in peace. As he had long since let his cook go, we had the same meal every day: lamb in mint sauce with crisps that he cooked to mush using a bain-marie.

At the weekends, I took the train to London. My mentor never came with me, as he despised the city. Here, Margaret Thatcher had ruled with an iron fist for two years, 'Fast Eddie' Davenport was yet to throw his wild, somewhat tacky parties in Kensington and Chelsea, and the City's enormous growth had only just begun. In Brixton, London's most troubled district, the arrest of a Black youth triggered clashes between police and demonstrators, and Mick Jagger was singing 'Emotional Rescue'. Everything was utterly brilliant and utterly miserable, everything was sacred and profane, and I believe I was happy then.

One evening I went to the cinema with a friend. We were keen to see *Raiders of the Lost Ark* – it was the big film of the moment, a new kind of adventure story, and Harrison Ford was great as Professor Henry Jones. At that point you were still allowed to smoke in cinemas and HD hadn't yet been invented, so by the time you got halfway through the film you could barely see anything through the smoke. It was the final screening of the day. After the credits had rolled we just sat there. There was a couple sitting in the front row, right up by the screen, in the seats where all you could make out were the colours. Suddenly the man got up. He swayed to and fro, pulled a wad of banknotes from his pocket, waved them in the air and shouted 'Again! Again!' into the empty auditorium. It was Mick Jagger. The projectionist went up to him, took the money, shook his head and ran the film a second time. We were allowed to stay, and it was wonderful.

A few years later I saw Jacques Deray's *La Piscine* for the first time, made back in 1968. Romy Schneider and Alain Delon are holidaying near Saint-Tropez, in a secluded house in the country. Nothing happens for the first few minutes. Slowness, inertia, the vast dry landscape beyond the house, the Mediterranean sun.

They kiss half-naked by the pool – blue-green water and dappled shade on the warm stone slabs. Then the phone rings. He tells her to ignore it and throws her into the pool. You're an idiot, she cries out, laughing, then answers the phone, and a short while later another couple pulls up in a russet Maserati Ghibli. Things get complicated and eventually there's a murder.

Remakes are nearly always a flop. The things we love simply can't be replicated. But there are exceptions. In 2016, Luca Guadagnino's *A Bigger Splash* came out, with Tilda Swinton in Romy Schneider's role. Swinton, referred to at one point in the film as the 'woman of the century', is a rock star recovering from vocal cord surgery, together with her boyfriend on an island off Sicily. The boyfriend is a bit tedious. Then Ralph Fiennes, Swinton's former lover, shows up. He wants her back. And he's full of life – charming, engaging and incredibly funny. In the middle of the film, he does a dance. The song: Mick Jagger's 'Emotional Rescue'. Fiennes deserved an Oscar for that scene alone. I suspect some of it was improvised. Fiennes looks right into the camera, his shirt open, wearing shorts – and he makes us happy. 'Emotional Rescue' – sometimes it's the music that saves us.

Romy Schneider and Alain Delon, Tilda Swinton and Ralph Fiennes, Mick Jagger singing, Harrison Ford in his hat – it's always a long, hot summer by the pool.

4

There's a documentary film on at the cinema about the lives of three lawyers: Otto Schily, Hans-Christian Ströbele and Horst Mahler. Three very different biographies: Schily became Federal Minister of the Interior, Ströbele a Green Party MP, and Mahler a right-wing extremist who ended up in prison. But in the 1970s, all three were lawyers defending 'German Autumn' terrorists – members of the Red Army Faction, or RAF – in criminal trials.

It all begins in 1967. During a demonstration outside the Deutsche Oper in Berlin, a policeman shoots a young man from behind at close range. The bullet shatters the student's skull; he falls to the ground, blood runs onto the pavement. A young woman kneels down beside him, puts her handbag under his head and screams for help. Two men carry the shot man to an ambulance on a stretcher. What happens next is wholly incomprehensible: rather than taking him to the nearby Albrecht-Achilles Hospital or to the neurosurgery department at the Virchow Clinic, the ambulance heads for Moabit A&E, which is much further away. It takes them an unusually long time to get there. When an orderly finally wheels the student into the operating theatre, all the anaesthetist can do is pronounce him dead.

Even now, the old television footage has lost none of its horror. As a viewer, you still feel stunned watching it. Ströbele says in the film that this was the day of his 'politicisation'. He's not alone: that day shaped almost an entire generation. After the student's death, the demonstrations escalated. The Chief of Police was forced to resign, followed by the Senator for the Interior and then the Mayor of West Berlin. But that wasn't the end. It was just the beginning.

The criminal proceedings against the policeman who shot Benno Ohnesorg became Schily's first 'political trial'. Mahler had arranged for him to represent the student's father, who was a joint plaintiff in the case. The policeman was acquitted. In the film, Schily speaks of something sinister surrounding the trial, of evidence that disappeared. Mahler says that for him, the trial was 'the confirmation of Marxist theory concerning the role of the state as an instrument of the ruling classes for the oppression of the exploited majority'. Yes, he really does talk like that.

Then we're shown images from the so-called 'Stammheim trials'. Ströbele calls the court building erected specifically for the trials 'a prejudgement cast in concrete'. We hear a tape recording of Schily's voice in the courtroom, bellowing: 'In the face of power, we posit arguments for the rule of law.' I know of no other lawyer who can spontaneously pull off that kind of sentence. The Stammheim police officers had wanted to frisk Schily, thereby infringing his status as a lawyer, an 'independent organ of the administration of justice'. That one sentence really tells you everything you need to know about Schily. *We posit arguments for the rule of law* – it is the leitmotif of his entire life.

All important social developments are mirrored in the criminal proceedings of their time. Disputes concerning the best way forward are always resolved before the courts, as well as by elections. In the trials of the RAF members, what was at stake was the constitutional state itself. Democracy in West Germany was young, and it was virtually helpless when confronted with terrorism. Politicians seemed unsure of how to respond. They acted in contradictory ways and made mistakes, and there was no clear constitutional stance in relation to the terrorist attacks.

In the course of their training, law students are taught the principle that the accused may not become the mere object of criminal proceedings. In a stable constitutional state, this goes without saying. But at the time, it was something that still had to be fought for in court. Hardly anyone wanted to recognise that terrorists are also human beings, that they too possess dignity. Schily, with Nazi corruption of the law still fresh in his mind, understood this. He believed in the rule of law and wanted to uphold it, even if that meant going up against the courts, up against the public prosecutor's office, and up against policemen who shoot demonstrators from behind. And so the law in and of itself became the focal point of Schily's thinking. And this is also why he was the most convincing of the lawyers: highly gifted, rhetorically brilliant, his every word pitch-perfect. Later, many were unable to fathom how this 'defender of terrorists', of all people, became Federal Minister of the Interior, but it was simply a logical step. Schily acted consistently – as he would see it – even as a minister: his only desire was to defend the law and the constitutional state, this great idea of humankind.

Ströbele is completely different. He feels personally affected if something is unjust, he says in the film. His sentences often have a moving quality about them. Shortly before the end of the film, he talks about himself. He often takes walks in the forest and likes to make jam. In his view, wars are always unjust. Listening to him, it suddenly seems quite easy to distinguish between good and evil. Ströbele sits with his white hair and bushy eyebrows in the courtroom, he's friendly and warm-hearted. The Jesuits at my boarding school would have called him a 'decent person' – he's a thoroughly likeable man. I wouldn't hesitate to trust him with my wallet and the keys to my apartment. But I would choose Schily to be my defence lawyer.

And Mahler? He's the most complicated of the three. He was a founding member of the RAF. In

1973, he was given a twelve-year prison sentence, which was increased to fourteen years in 1974. When the leader of the Berlin Christian Democrats was kidnapped by RAF terrorists in 1975, to force the release of 'captured comrades', Mahler was the only one who voluntarily stayed in prison. He was released in 1980. Later, he was repeatedly convicted of inciting racial hatred. He treated every courtroom like a stage and took to threatening judges with the death penalty in a future Fourth Reich. He became a Holocaust denier and greeted one interviewer with the words 'Heil Hitler'. In the film, you see him at Nazi rallies saying crazy stuff – he just doesn't seem to care anymore.

When Mahler was imprisoned in 1970, Ströbele looked after his family, while Schily sent the complete works of Hegel to him in prison. That's also typical of the two lawyers. Mahler – so it's said in judicial circles – then spent a decade reading nothing but Hegel.

Hegel created the most self-contained of all philosophical systems. He organised the whole of reality according to his theories, and, as with any significant ideology, reading him can suck you in. I believe that if a highly intelligent man studies Hegel for ten years in a prison cell, then this man will become what

Mahler became. Mahler is the cold, untouchable intellectual who gets caught up in every last ramification of a theory and eventually perishes there. These kind of individuals feature time and again in German history, and they're often lawyers. Whether they are right- or left-wing extremists is completely irrelevant. Mahler became a prisoner of himself.

The film tells a story about our complicated country. Three young men, three fundamentally different characters, three very different political life choices. Schily defended the law against the state, Ströbele believed in the power of good, Mahler got tangled up in extremes. The three lawyers are old men today, they have lived their lives.

At the end of the film, each of them talks about the others. Mahler says that Schily views him as 'political filth', but that he considers this 'to be an honour'. Then he grins into the camera. The scene in which Schily is asked about Mahler is one of the standout scenes of the film. Schily raises his hands and says: 'A tragedy.' Nothing else.

*

As I write this, I'm sitting in a café outside the court where the Mahler trial took place in 1973. It's autumn now, the leaves have been raked into piles and it's rained continuously for a week. Of course, big trials still take place and always will, but everybody in the justice system learned lessons from the Stammheim trials. The Criminal Procedure Code was pushed to its absolute limits for the first time, but equally, it was during these trials that the constitutional state found its feet. The battle for the dignity of the accused is still being waged today – it has to be, on a daily basis – but lots of things have also become easier. Perhaps that's the real achievement of the Stammheim trial lawyers.

I don't remember every detail of the film, but there's one bit I can't forget. It offers a fitting response to Mahler's aberrations. On 13 March 1997, Schily is standing at a lectern before the German Bundestag. The subject is an exhibition: 'War of Annihilation: Crimes of the Wehrmacht, 1941–1944'. Schily can barely speak. He falters, apologises, is close to tears. Then he talks about his brothers, about the victims of war, and about the Nazis. I can't recall the last time a speech moved me so.

5

Smoking has been banned for years inside Moabit Criminal Court. In the corridors, yellow paper signs are taped to the tiled walls: 'Visitor smoking area in the Gallows Courtyard'. The defendant smokes anyway. He's standing just behind the door to the court, on the steps leading to the prison cells. The officer on duty gets annoyed and tells him to stop. The defendant carries on smoking, completely unruffled. He's been on remand for six months, awaiting trial for manslaughter. He looks at the officer, gives a shrug and says: 'What you gonna do? Arrest me?'

On 22 April 1947, Wehmeyer sets off from Berlin in a northerly direction together with a friend. There's hardly anything to eat in the bombed-out capital and the two men are hungry. They're planning to barter some clothing for potatoes – Wehmeyer has a pair of boots and some trousers with him. These kinds of black-market trades were called 'Hamstergeschäfte' or 'hamster deals', and they were often the only way to survive.

Wehmeyer is twenty-three years old. He lives with his mother and sisters in a disused railway carriage. His father died shortly after returning from a Russian prisoner-of-war camp. Wehmeyer began an apprenticeship as a locksmith, stole a chisel and was sacked. After that he got by with poorly paid odd jobs, a precarious existence with no future.

On the road, the two men meet a woman. She's sixty-one, and like them has travelled to the countryside to barter some goods. By chance, they cross paths again that evening. Wehmeyer hasn't had any luck: he didn't manage to trade his items. The woman was more successful: she's now the owner of a sack of potatoes – twenty kilos, a small fortune in those days. The three of them load the sack onto a handcart and head back to Berlin. It starts to get dark. Suddenly, without any warning, Wehmeyer punches the woman. His fist strikes her on the neck, breaking her larynx, and she falls to the ground. He ties her hands behind her back, stuffs a handkerchief in her mouth, pulls down her underwear and rapes her. His friend looks on and does nothing to intervene. Later, he'll say that he was afraid of Wehmeyer. The gag stops the woman from getting any air. She suffocates while Wehmeyer rapes her. Once Wehmeyer is done, he takes the dead woman's potatoes.

Five days later, the woman's body is discovered in a field. Wehmeyer and his friend are swiftly identified. At the police station, each accuses the other. A court-appointed expert questions Wehmeyer, subsequently noting that the young man had always been 'selfish and callous'.

The trial lasts just one day. The public prosecutor makes reference to a previous conviction for robbery – Wehmeyer had snatched a woman's handbag when he was sixteen years old.

The judges quickly reach agreement. The verdict states: 'The accused, through his gruesome deed, has disqualified himself from the company of civilised people and forfeited his right to life.'

That's how things sounded back then, two years after the end of the war.

Wehmeyer's lawyer tries to save him. He files applications, tries to win some time, does everything he can. All in vain. The judges don't want to hear it; they reject every single application. They know they won't get to sentence people to death for very much longer.

On 11 May 1949, the guillotine severs Wehmeyer's head from his torso. It's the final execution to take place in Moabit. Twelve days later the Grundgesetz, Germany's new constitution, comes into force and the death penalty is abolished.

The night before the execution, in his cell, Wehmeyer is said to have smoked continuously.

6

In 1973, a bathtub that Joseph Beuys had swathed in gauze bandages and plasters is cleaned by two members of a local Social Democratic Party association so they can use it to wash up some glasses. The damages for the ruined artwork come to 40,000 DM.

In 1974, a manufacturer of household products puts out an advert in which two cleaning ladies are shown scrubbing a bathtub in a museum of modern art.

In 1986, Joseph Beuys's *Fat Corner* is thrown in the bin by a janitor at the Düsseldorf Academy of Art. Once again, the damages come to 40,000 DM.

In 2014, three artists turn the remnants of *Fat Corner* into schnapps. The artists sample the alcohol and say it tastes like Parmesan cheese. The rest of the distillate is exhibited in a glass bottle.

In 2011, in a museum in Dortmund, a plastic tub by Martin Kippenberger is comprehensively scrubbed by a cleaning lady. The size of the damages remains unknown.

7

A former fellow pupil from my boarding school comes to one of my readings in southern Germany. I don't recognise him. He was two years above me – we were twelve and fourteen at the time. I was an 'Internal' there, as it was known. 'Externals' were children from the surrounding villages who just attended the school in the mornings and weren't boarders.

His father was a forester, a short, dark man with a full black beard and a curiously high voice. I went over to their house one time. The family ate dinner in silence. In the corner of the small living room, above an oak bench, was a crucified Jesus in a glass case. I'd never heard the word *Herrgottswinkel* – 'our Lord God's corner' – before.

After dinner, I thanked his mother. It tasted very good, I said. Her mouth was a white line in her yellow face: 'One doesn't say that food tastes good. All food is good.'

My schoolmate was a gentle boy with dark eyes. He excelled in every subject, and the girls really liked him. Once, he came to school with a black eye; he said he'd bumped into something. Another time, in the changing rooms during gym class, we saw that his back was covered in bloody welts. There came a point when I lost track of him.

After the reading, he invites me over for dinner. We drive through the forest to his house. He barely says a word, which is unlike before. His car smells of wet dogs and tree resin. When we get out, he wordlessly takes a rifle from the boot and slings it over his shoulder. Only now do I recognise everything again: he is living in his father's house and has become a forester, just like him.

8

Imre Kertész died today. He lived in an apartment above my chambers. We would cross paths
occasionally in the slow-moving lift, and discuss
literature, opera and the restaurants in our street.

At some point, he asked me to sort out a small legal
matter for him. After completing it, I wanted to save
him the trouble of coming to the office, so I took the
papers up to him. It was around eight in the evening.
He opened the door, elegantly dressed as always – fine
shoes, a cashmere jacket, an old, very heavy scent –
and invited me in. He was living alone at that point;
his wife only visited rarely. I didn't know that he was
already so ill. In his living room, he had laid a table
with a white tablecloth, silver cutlery, crystal glasses,
two candles. I asked if he was expecting company, I
didn't wish to intrude. No, no, he said, it was

something he did every evening. One 'mustn't let oneself go, after all'.

Kertész knew everything there was to know about death. He had been in the concentration camps of Auschwitz, Buchenwald and Tröglitz/Rehmsdorf. He had survived, liberated in 1945 at the age of just sixteen. He once said: 'I think I have already experienced every one of my moments. It is over, and I am still here.'

To love oneself, that's too much to ask. But we should maintain a certain form. It's our final foothold.

9

In Zurich, I meet with a judge who sits on the Swiss supreme court. We talk about the death penalty, about the gradual erosion of our last red lines. He says that it's easy to change the constitution in Switzerland. They've already held referendums on criminal law – for example on the issue of 'lifelong custody'. Law professors, the judiciary and enlightened society had all been united in their views at the time, but the people had voted differently.

The judge is a calm, level-headed man. He often asks himself what the 'rule of law' actually means. What would he do if a majority in his country passed a law that reintroduced the death penalty? When should a principle-based decision take precedence over a majority decision? When must it do so? Or do ethics count for nothing against the will of the people?

And, if in fact they do, who gets to determine what these ethics are?

America, 1893: Will Purvis is sentenced to death for the murder of a man. The circumstances are complex – they involve an organisation similar to the Ku Klux Klan, internal feuding and a deadly sniper shot.

At the trial, Purvis claims to be innocent, but the jury doesn't believe his alibi witnesses. As he's led from the courtroom, he shouts at those sitting in judgement upon him: 'You'll all die before me. I'll live longer than the lot of you.'

On 7 February 1894, the hangman places a rope around Purvis's neck in front of hundreds of eager onlookers. He releases the trapdoor, but the knot comes undone and Purvis survives unscathed. He's returned to prison. Shortly afterwards, the Mississippi Supreme Court rules that Purvis should be hanged again.

The night before the execution, he escapes from prison. Three years later (by which time a new governor has taken office), he is pardoned. Purvis marries and has seven children. Twenty-four years later, another man confesses to the murder for which

Purvis was convicted. Purvis receives five thousand dollars' compensation, an enormous sum then.

In 1938, Purvis dies peacefully, an old man in the bosom of his family. And he was right: three days earlier, the last of the twelve jurors – those who'd sentenced him to hang forty-five years previously – had drawn his final breath.

The judge in Zurich sits and thinks for a long time. In the end, he says that he would resign. A law that permitted the death penalty wasn't one he could support.

10

The editor-in-chief of a so-called lifestyle magazine asks if I'd like to come along to a fashion show in Paris. Maybe I could write a little something about it. It's the high point of Fashion Week there, an extraordinary 'event', she says – because everyone talks like that in her world. It's the greatest honour to be there, practically impossible to get a ticket, you have to have 'connections'. She shows me the invitation on overly thick card that she's been carrying around in her handbag for days. The words *Haute Couture* are drawn on it in childish handwriting.

Ernest Hemingway wrote that Paris is a moveable feast at the end of the 1950s, and it became his most joyful book. He had lived in the city in the

1920s, meeting Gertrude Stein, James Joyce, Ezra Pound, Ford Madox Ford, John Dos Passos and F. Scott Fitzgerald. It was here that he became a writer. When he left, Hemingway is said to have forgotten a suitcase containing diaries and notebooks at the Hôtel Ritz. It was only when he revisited Paris in 1956 and a waiter unexpectedly retrieved the suitcase from the cellar that he was able to write the book. Now he had experience gained from an entire lifetime of writing as well as the fresh memories of his youth. I don't know if it's true, but perhaps where good stories are concerned that's pretty much beside the point anyway.

When I was young, you were still allowed to smoke in cafés. I lived in a tiny room, which was pricey and in a dreadful condition. A large Senegalese prostitute rented the apartment next to mine. We got on well, but her working hours always lasted until five or six in the morning, and she and her clients were so loud that I could barely sleep. She would often invite me over first thing, and we would drink awful but cheap instant coffee. She'd tell me about her clients and their strange requests, and show me photos of her large family, to whom she sent almost all of her money.

I spoke hardly any French, but that didn't matter, because she talked enough for both of us, and we were less lonely that way. My room had only a small fan heater and got awfully cold in winter – the windows froze shut and ice flowers formed on the thin glass panes.

Back then I had no money and would sit for hours in cheap cafés. I don't know if it's because I was in Paris at an age when one is shaped by places and everything was new to me, but I still dream of that city, of its smells and colours, of my friends, of the time when we believed everything would work out for us because we knew so little and because reality didn't have a hold over us yet. I think of all this when the editor-in-chief invites me along, and I say yes.

Even getting there is horrible. There are miles of traffic jams – the drive from the airport takes an hour and a half. I meet the editor-in-chief at the Café de Flore. Everyone here seems to belong to the fashion industry. They're constantly looking around in case they recognise anyone or anyone recognises them. They snap Instagram and Facebook photos on their mobiles: they take pictures of the food and the serviettes and even the little packets of sugar lying on the saucers.

Hemingway's café was on the Place Saint-Michel, not far from the Boulevard Saint-Germain and the Café de Flore where we're sitting. I would rather be there. These are the most beautiful days of the year. It's grown cooler beneath the sycamore trees, at night the lights from the cafés and illuminated shops are reflected on the pavements, and the air already smells of autumn. This city seems to survive everything – the Hollywood love stories, the Eiffel Tower kitsch, and even the permanently empty fifty-million-euro apartments owned by Arabs and Russians.

When you're writing, you talk to the people you invent, you live their lives with them, and at a certain point, the times between writing become unimportant, the writing becomes what's real. The same is true of the Café Deux Magots and even of the Café de Flore, in spite of these people, in spite of Paris Fashion Week and in spite of the Instagram photos. It works if you're on your own and manage to keep to yourself.

The following day we take a taxi to the Grand Palais, where hundreds of people are queueing in the hope of getting tickets. The Palais interior is over forty metres high. The roof is made of glass, edged with riveted, iron struts painted a pale green. This is where, at the dawn of the previous century, women in summer dresses and men in light-coloured suits attended the first automobile exhibitions and believed in progress. Life would become easier and more interesting, they thought then, in the short time remaining before the great wars.

The décor for the haute couture show is perfect: literary quotations on the walls and floor, everything painted a dazzling white, the whole hall like an overexposed photograph. Waiters serve sugar biscuits on silver trays, but of course no one eats anything here. The world's super-rich and beautiful and famous sit on white, lacquered wooden boxes, and when a pregnant woman is photographed, she immediately turns to the side so that it's clear she's expecting a baby and isn't just fat.

The start of the show is deafeningly loud – a leaden, hammering rhythm whose pounding makes the stomach lurch. The models appear wearing sombre make-up. They look like the Erinyes, the Greek goddesses of vengeance. None of the women smiles. Their gait is grotesque – their hips are pushed so far forward, I'm afraid they'll fall over. The young women seem terribly strained, like streetwalkers without breasts or bottoms. After twelve minutes, it's all over. Later, someone tells me that the models consume only ice cubes and cotton wool balls dipped briefly in orange juice.

All of this is a misunderstanding. Fashion is an illusion, a happy promise. Of course, it's not a promise that's ever kept, but it needs to be bright and cheery and light. I wanted to admire women and see chic dresses. I had hoped for beauty, elegance and perfection. But this was just a sterile, twelve-minute ballet laid on by a company worth billions. After the show, each guest receives a gift bag containing shower gel and bath products in black packaging. I give mine to a woman outside the Palais who hadn't managed to get a ticket.

On the flight home, I think of the Ringelnatz poem:

Gift me your heart for a fortnight,
you long-striding giraffe child,
that I may openly, as into the wind,

tell you things both good and dear.
When I saw you, O lanky Gabriele,
a hole in your stocking moved me,
and without you knowing, my soul
greeted you through this hole.
Don't drive it away, say: Yes!
It was so wonderful, when I saw you.

II

She spends the night in a village on the Atlantic coast. She drove the whole way here alone, almost sixteen hours in her small car. She's cried a lot over the last few days.

The hotel is pokey, the room is stuffy, she can't sleep. She gets dressed again and wanders through the town. The cafés and restaurants have been closed for hours. There are plaques on some of the houses – fifty years ago, painters and writers lived here. 'Due to the light', it said in the hotel brochure on the bed-side table. She reads the names of the dead artists on the house walls.

She's still wondering if she did the right thing. She'd simply left, even though he'd been kind to her all these years, loving. He had taken care of her, organised her life, looked out for her. Nothing about him was wrong – he was her home, a good person, much better than her. There are no explanations, no words, nothing substantial she can hold on to.

For a while, she sits on a stone bench by the harbour – the smell of decay, the slap of the brackish water against the quay walls, the damp salt on her skin. She remembers how they visited the sea a few years ago, not far from here. Early one morning they saw a deer swimming in the water, the animal's raised head between the golden waves, panic-stricken and crazed. She had told him then that he didn't know who she was, and that the images in his head were just his images, not her.

Eventually she gets tired and turns back. On the second floor of the hotel a woman is standing on the balcony. She is naked and smoking a cigarette. The woman on the balcony looks at her and nods, the fellowship of insomniacs. A man steps onto the balcony behind her. He cups her breasts; she bursts into bright laughter and clasps her hands over his. Then she lets the cigarette fall, turns to him and disappears into the darkness of the room.

The woman goes to her room, lies fully clothed on the bed and instantly falls asleep. After a few hours, she wakes up in a sweat, her clothes sticking to her body. She opens the door to the small balcony. It has finally rained, the air is fresh and cool. Even without the gift of being happy there's a duty to live, she thinks now.

12

Lars Gustafsson was a Swedish writer. He won prestigious literary prizes, his books were translated into all the major languages, and for many years he was considered a candidate for the Nobel Prize.

In the seventies, he wrote a book called *The Tennis Players*. In it, a Swedish professor accepts a position at the University of Texas in Austin to teach philosophy and literature. The professor is pale, thin, tired and not very sporty. He likes the American students – their curiosity and their uncomplicated, easy manner. They're quite different to their European counterparts, he thinks. His English isn't very good yet: he translates Nietzsche's 'Übermensch' as 'Superman' and this leads to complications. In the New World, far from the darkness of Sweden, in the heat of Austin, he gradually begins to change. In the course of the book, he becomes a first-class tennis player. And gains his freedom.

Lars Gustafsson really did teach philosophy and literature in Austin. In 1983, he did a book tour through Europe. I attended one of his readings in Constance, and afterwards asked him if he fancied a game of tennis. He said yes.

I collected him the following morning, a bright blue midsummer's day. Our court was at the front of the park. It was extremely hot on the red clay. In the breaks between games, we stood by the edge of the court in the dark green shade of the old chestnut trees and elms. Gustafsson's movements were a bit stiff, but he played with high concentration and had a good hard stroke.

Later, we went swimming. I asked if he found his events gruelling. He laughed and told me about a reading he had given in Sweden, in a tiny village miles out in the country. Shortly after he'd set off, a storm blew up: it began snowing heavily and a few minutes later the road was completely blanketed with snow. Gustafsson thought about turning back, but was already too far into his journey. Eventually, he reached the village.

Sweden is a very affluent country and spends lots of money on culture, so even this remote spot had a huge community hall with a proper stage and seating for twelve hundred people. Gustafsson slipped twice in the car park before finally making it to the entrance. Inside it was bright and warm, but the hall was completely empty. Apart from the front row, that is, where a lone man was seated. The last thing Gustafsson wanted to do now was to go back to the car. And in any case, he told himself, this man was also here in spite of the terrible weather. So he pulled himself together, got onstage, stood at the lectern and began to read.

He somehow even felt a bit proud of himself now, like a saviour of literature. Yes, he said to himself, it's quite right to read for just one person – after all, he could be fiction's very last friend. So he made a big effort, even though it also seemed rather absurd to him. Nonetheless, he gave the same reading he had already given to thousands of people in New York, Paris, Rome and Berlin.

As he spoke, he kept thinking that he had seen the man in the front row somewhere before, but wasn't quite able to place him.

After an hour and a half, he drew his reading to a close. The man in the front row clapped politely. Gustafsson bowed, left the stage and walked through the hall towards the door. At the final moment, he saw the other man go onstage, pull the microphone towards him, take some sheets of paper from his briefcase and begin to speak. It was now that Gustafsson finally recognised him: he was the other famous writer invited to that evening's event.

We sat by the swimming pool under the faded blue-and-white wooden roof, and drank iced tea. Gustafsson talked about the winters in Sweden and the heat of Austin, and then we discussed the tennis serve. In his view, it was a miracle: even the greatest players in the world could miss the ball six times in a row. No one knows why it happens, he said, there's no logical explanation. The tennis serve is just as complex as the question of how we might lead successful lives.

Much later, I read in one of his poems how he wanted to die.

It should be a day in early August
the swallows gone, but a bumblebee
still around, practising its arc
in the raspberry shade.
A light, but not stubborn wind
should be passing over the August meadows.

You should be there,
but not say a great deal,
just stroke my hair a little
and look me in the eyes
with that little smile
right in the corner of your eye.
And then I'd like,
not without a sense of relief,
to see this world disappear.

On 2 April 2016, in the early evening, a light drizzle began to fall in Västerås. That night, the sky was overcast. The following day, a Sunday, was dry with a maximum temperature of eleven degrees. The wind speed was six kilometres an hour – the Met Office noted a 'light breeze'. There were no summer meadows as yet, but spring blossom starts appearing in the vastness of Västerås in April, and with it,

the bumblebee queens awaken from their winter
sleep.

It is time to go home.
But we are already home.

Lars Gustafsson died on 3 April 2016.

13

The owner of a stationery shop shows me some colouring books for adults. They're the latest big thing. They're selling so well that a manufacturer of pencils and colouring pencils has been running extra night shifts for weeks now to meet the ever-growing demand.

Those buying the colouring books, says the shop owner, claim that colouring brings them 'peace'. One person even told him it 'slows down everyday life'. That sounds strange, of course, but at the time a colouring book is number four on Amazon's best-seller list. In any case, he says, it's excellent business for him as a shop owner supplying paper goods, because only wealthy people do this kind of thing. His customers always want the most expensive pencils and the most expensive colouring books.

He shows me the 'Albrecht Dürer Wooden Case'. It contains a hundred and twenty 'artists'' watercolour pencils' with 'unsurpassed lightfastness and vibrant colour'. His top-selling item, however, is the 'Berlin Colouring Poster' – on four square metres of the very finest paper. It constantly sells out and he can't restock fast enough. Friends and acquaintances meet up for dinner and then colour in the poster together.

It has rained briefly, and outside the stationer's there's a scent of lime blossom, petrol, and wet asphalt drying in the sun. A few doors down is a bookshop. The hardback edition of *A Supposedly Fun Thing I'll Never Do Again* by David Foster Wallace is on display in the window. It costs twenty euros. The 'Alps' colouring book for adults is seven euros more.

llem Lisbon the business nor in Dortmund behind
trunche of cocaine found unbilt sleaping in the
his over the campu wolle. The were prisoner roce in
while innocent of people died. Criminals were
tortured and killed by local cartel syndicate, their
bodies then minced and turned into the sewers.

14

A few years ago, I had to make a trip to Brazil. A
client had been arrested there after trying to
smuggle several hundred kilos of cocaine into Europe.
Transporting drugs in such huge quantities is complicated. The first rule of professional criminals –
commit crimes alone and don't tell anyone – can't
really be upheld during these sorts of transactions.
Either my client hadn't paid a member of his own
organisation enough or he hadn't threatened them
enough. Someone had betrayed him and he'd spent
the last six months sitting in a prison in Rio de Janeiro.

This prison was a nasty place. Dirty water pooled
on the stone floors, the prisoners sat on wooden beds
with their legs drawn up, and it stank like a cesspit.
The cells were designed for eight inmates, but housed
twenty or thirty men. The toilet was just a hole in the

floor. Lots of the inmates were ill. Their teeth fell out, patches of eczema formed on their skin, big insects ran over the damp walls. There were frequent riots in which hundreds of people died. Prisoners were tortured and killed by local crime syndicates, their bodies dismembered and flushed into the sewers.

I was staying at the Copacabana Palace, a pleasant 1920s hotel right on the beach. Marlene Dietrich, Orson Welles, Igor Stravinsky and Stefan Zweig had all stayed there for a while. The hotel had a swimming pool and a terrace overlooking the sea. I sat there for hours with interpreters and local lawyers, drawing up defence strategies and discussing ways to extradite our client to Europe. It was bizarre. We had a view of the most famous beach in the world. On the white sand, beneath parasols, were little bars. Men with oiled bodies performed martial arts sequences and played footvolley; many of the young women wore the skimpy swimwear that locals called 'Fio dental' – 'dental floss'. But here we were discussing prison mortality rates and Brazil's bewildering legal system.

On my final day, I was sitting on the terrace by myself, trying to understand the court rulings with the help of a Portuguese-English dictionary from the hotel library. I was drinking iced tea and eating toast with slices of cold cucumber when a fat man in a wrinkled linen suit approached my table. He greeted me warmly by name, but I didn't recognise him.

'Don't you remember me?' he asked, laughing. His German was flawless, with just a slight English accent.

'Forgive me . . .'

'No, no, it's OK,' he interjected. 'It's true I'm a bit out of shape now,' he said, and patted his stomach. And then he gave his name: 'Harold.'

At that moment it all came back to me. I had met Harold over thirty years earlier at a wedding; a second cousin of his had married a friend of mine. The couple split up two years later – Harold called it a 'marriage of errors'. At the time, he was studying brewery management, German and philosophy in Munich – a combination he viewed as 'entirely natural'.

I had visited him a few times in the north of England during the university holidays. His family lived in an eighteenth-century castle known simply as 'The House'. Harold reckoned that The House had 'roughly a hundred and twenty rooms', but of course he'd never counted them.

He was an only child. The plan was for him to inherit his father's title, The House, the landscaped gardens, the farming and forestry businesses, the breweries and the fish farms. The family was related to Bertrand Russell and the Mitford sisters, and he would joke about his place in the royal line of succession. Much later, a philosophy tutor in Munich told me that Harold was the most gifted student he'd ever had. It was true that he possessed a brilliant mind, but he also lacked any ambition. Exerting oneself was foolish, he said. In the holidays, we spent entire days lying on the roof of The House eating strawberries while he related yet another anecdote about his family.

Harold joined me at my table. His skin was red from the sun, his formerly blond hair was now white. He waved over a waiter.

'Are you here on holiday?' I asked.

'I live here – it's been about two years now,' he said. 'Got kind of stranded. The food and climate are good, and I like the sea. Not particularly keen on the beach, though.'

I asked after his family. His father had died a few years ago, he said. 'After twenty-five years of marriage, my mother buggered off with another man. An investment banker or riding instructor or something.'

Harold's father had worn a three-piece suit every day, but I had never seen him in any footwear other than black wellingtons.

'And why aren't you in England?'

'Well,' he said, and ordered a cold Brahma beer. 'The divorce ruined my father. Not financially – there were contracts for that – but in every other way. He probably wasn't very nice to her when they were married, but after she left he started drinking. And then . . .'

The waiter brought him his beer. Condensation was forming on the glass.

'. . . and then he signed over The House and the land to the National Trust. I still have a lifelong right to live in four rooms. But everything's been tidied up and it's not very nice anymore. Coachloads of visitors every day. They pay four pounds twenty pence admission, and buy postcards and key rings of The House.'

'Why did he do that?'

'Well, I'm the last of the line, there probably won't be anyone after me. I might well have had to do it myself at some point – perhaps he just wanted to spare me.'

I told him about a morning at his house. I had got up early, the lawn was still damp, there was a rainy grey-green light. The boat shed was full of forgotten things: an axe with a broken handle, dried-out paint in cans, a life ring with a damaged throw-line. Light blue paint had peeled away from the wood of the boat. I rowed out onto the lake. It was quiet and cold. Then, high above, the loud calls of greylag geese. There must have been hundreds of them. I had never seen anything like it.

'Oh yes, the greylag geese,' said Harold. 'I think of them often. They fly to Africa, guided by the earth's magnetic field. *Nocturnal travellers*, my father called them.'

'Don't you miss all that?'

Harold gave this some thought. In his face, I now saw the young man he'd once been.

'I don't think so, my dear,' he said after a while. 'No. *Heimat* isn't a place, it's our memories.'

Later, Harold took me for dinner at his friends' house. It soon became too much for me, so I ordered a taxi back to the hotel. I got out at the beach and walked along the illuminated promenade with its wavy black-and-white marble pattern. The temperature had cooled again, the sea was calm. All of a sudden, I thought of my father. He's standing barefoot in the river, fishing. He's wearing a faded straw hat and there's a cigarette in the corner of his mouth. He's slim and tall and bronzed, the sleeves of his white shirt are rolled up, his glass watch face keeps winking in the sun. There's a smell of freshly cut grass. He's given me a red Swiss army knife, I'm six or seven years old. I sit on a stone and sharpen branches with it. When he catches a couple of trout, we rub them with salt, spear them on the sticks and hold them over the fire. My hands are black and sticky from the tree resin – even in the river I have trouble getting it off. My father says you can make pitch from resin. He tells me about a physicist in Australia who wanted to know how fast pitch flows. He filled a glass funnel with some heated pitch, let it set for three years, then cut the funnel's stem. It took eight years for the first drop to fall, another nine years for the second drop to fall, and then the scientist died. But the funnel still exists, the experiment continues.

The trouts' eyes turn white in the heat of the fire. The fish are full of bones and taste awful, but we pretend they're a delicacy. We decide to go to Australia to see the next drop fall. We'll visit the Aborigines, my father says. They know only the present – no past and no future, their language doesn't have words for those. We'll have to ask what they think about the flow-rate of pitch and they'll let us in on the secret. We look into the fire and think about the slowest experiment in the world.

Back then there was no time, in the way that memories have no time. It was just the summer when we were down by the river, catching trout, and I thought that nothing would ever change.

Today, I'm older than the age my father reached – he died early and we never did get to Australia.

Half a century has passed since then, and everything has changed. The big households have been dissolved, and with them the maids and the cooks have disappeared, the gardeners, the chauffeurs and the forester whose dogs I loved. The dark green park I grew up in has long since been sold. The ponds with the water lilies and the curved wooden bridge, the tennis court of red clay that clung to my white trousers and shoes, the swimming pool where leaves drifted on bright blue water, the orangery, the weathered garden nursery, the stables – all this no longer exists. Harold was right: the slow days of my childhood, the smoke of my father's cigarettes, the amber light of the soft summer evenings – that world lives only in me now.

The next morning, the hotel concierge handed me a thick envelope. Harold wrote that he wasn't able to come down for breakfast, he'd had too much to drink, and wished me a good trip home. In the envelope was a book – I don't know where he'd dug it up – an old edition of Eichendorff's poems. Much later, on the night flight back to Europe, I thought of the *nocturnal travellers* and leafed through the book. Harold had placed a hideous postcard of The House between its pages. He had marked two lines of a poem, and these now always come to my mind whenever anyone speaks of *Heimat*:

> *We yearn for home*
> *and don't know, where to go?*

15

Telekom has named its new phone tariffs 'Magenta'. They're better value for money than before, says the woman on the phone – a 'truly combative price'.

Magenta is a small town in Lombardy, a few miles from the outskirts of Milan. Here, in 1859, Sardinia-Piedmont and Napoleon III went into combat against the Austrian emperor. At stake: supremacy in Northern Italy. On 4 June 1859, so many soldiers were slaughtered in battle that the earth turned red. The name of the colour 'magenta' is said to have originated there.

16

Mark Twain supposedly said that he'd forgo a place in heaven if he wasn't allowed to smoke there. He was right. After all, things only got interesting when Adam and Eve ate the fruit from the tree of knowledge and were expelled from Paradise. At last, an end to this interminable boredom, to the vacuousness and perpetual delight. The two became human, and only then saw the world and themselves clearly. They paid for it by becoming mortal – that's just how things were with the Old Testament God, all or nothing. And that's why Helmut Schmidt seemed to me to be the ideal smoker. For isn't every cigarette – and in his case it's likely to have been well over a million – basically a 'memento mori', a reminder that we're going to die, which in turn is a constant reminder we're alive? This was him to a T. He had a quadruple bypass and a pacemaker. But like a true gambler, who needs to lose to keep on playing, he probably wouldn't have enjoyed smoking if it hadn't been so terribly bad for him. That's also why developing a healthy cigarette or using nicotine patches and gum (except on long flights, perhaps) is all wrong. And as for quitting smoking – seriously? For ages, I worried that Schmidt's doctors might yet convince him to give up. Another great smoker – Zeno Cosini, the hero of Italo Svevo's novel – spends 640 pages trying to stop. When he manages it after the umpteenth time, he says: 'So I was completely cured, but incurably ridiculous!'

Of course, Helmut Schmidt was never ridiculous, even though he smoked 'Reyno White' – an ultra-white cigarette, a hundred millimetres long with just a thin green band up by the filter. It's actually a bit feminine, and frankly tastes pretty awful as well: the menthol spoils the tobacco. But he smoked it with great elegance and often openly celebrated the process. He had the ability to interrupt any conversation for a few seconds with his concentrated lighting-up ritual and wonderfully arrogant exhalation of smoke over other people's heads. It was a performance in which everything came together: his poise, his condescension, his analyses and prophecies, which it has to be said weren't always right, and his Caesar's head.

Schmidt smoked constantly, and when he didn't, he took snuff. People often say that the best cigarette is the one you have right after sex. That isn't true, of course: the post-coital cigarette has just the same value as all the others. Cigarettes are a smoker's allies. They accompany him in his triumphs, they're with him in his defeats, and they never let him down. I imagine Schmidt smoking his first cigarette after it was confirmed he would be chancellor. Or when he had to make the life-or-death choice involving kidnapped industrialist Hanns-Martin Schleyer. I'm sure he smoked at that moment, too, and it helped him to face the terrible loneliness of his decision.

Schmidt used disposable lighters and extracted his cigarettes straight from the pack. That always amazed me. I have a silver cigarette case, which once belonged to my father, and a tortoiseshell lighter. These kinds of accessories are important: the bright click of the lighter, the weight of the silver, the way the case springs open – all of this offers protection against the ugliness and brutality of the world. But maybe a politician has to make these sorts of concessions.

Like the silly Prince Heinrich peaked cap Schmidt wore, which didn't remotely match his immaculate suits.

Now Helmut Schmidt is dead and smoking is banned everywhere. You couldn't ever imagine Angela Merkel smoking on a talk show or sniffing snuff. People say that smoking no longer fits the age we live in, that it causes cancer and heart disease, ages the skin and harms the environment. That's all true, I think, and light a cigarette. And then, while I smoke, I think of Jean-Luc Godard's *Breathless*. I still remember the first time I saw it, in Rome, in a tiny basement cinema to mark its twenty-fifth anniversary. In the opening sequence, Jean-Paul Belmondo is already smoking, and he keeps going for the entire film. In the final scene, when he's running down the street after having been shot, he's still smoking. After collapsing, he takes one last drag before the cigarette falls from his mouth and rolls away over the cobblestones. In a barely audible voice, he tells his gorgeous lover Jean Seberg that she 'makes him want to puke', then smiles at her and dies.

Yes, of course, we need to stop smoking and live sensibly. And we should no longer consume sugar or meat – absolutely. That was the great thing about Helmut Schmidt: none of this stuff interested him in the slightest.

17

President Donald Trump was no match for Pokémon Go: the smartphone game was the world's most frequently googled search term in 2016. Apple's iPhone 7 came second, with Trump having to settle for third place. This isn't something he's in the habit of doing. When he visited the Queen in London and inspected the Guard of Honour with her, he walked a step ahead of the old lady.

According to court protocol, the Queen's husband Prince Philip, then ninety-seven, was always required to walk behind her at official functions.

18

We meet at Potsdamer Platz in the middle of Berlin. The Sony Center's roof is modelled on Mount Fuji, the holy Japanese mountain where the gods reside and are said to watch over us. We have a coffee. There are hundreds of people in the plaza – you can buy mobile phones, jewellery, newspapers and souvenirs. Or get your eyes lasered.

From here, it's less than fourteen hundred kilometres to Kyiv. The flight-time is only two hours, but it's a totally different world. The lawyer is in her mid-thirties. A slender woman in a lightweight dress, she has an air of vulnerability about her. But she's taken them all on: the so-called People's Republics of Donetsk and Luhansk, the paramilitary units, the Russian Federation and Putin himself. She tells me about the torture going on in her country: there are over seventy-five cellars in the provinces where men and women have been tortured and killed, or carted off and caged like animals. The rapes, the torture, the murders – all are systematically carried out in order to break the resistance. Eastern Ukraine is to become a Russian province. 'Fundamental rights,' says the lawyer, 'are non-existent where we are. Not even the basic principles of law apply anymore.' She says that her organisation can do nothing more than document the crimes. She has seen how the blood is washed off the cellar walls, how the lists of those killed are destroyed and the death warrants burned. Even torturers know there's no statute of limitations for crimes against humanity. At some point, evidence is necessary to make sense of the past.

A child on a scooter bumps into the table next to us, and a man's triple-decker ice cream falls into his lap. He swears. We have to laugh, and for a moment the lawyer looks as though she has a perfectly normal life. 'Why can't it always be like this?' she asks.

We talk about our families' pasts. Her Jewish grandparents were deported from Vienna by the Nazis and later murdered. Her mother was able to flee, and was taken in by distant relatives, farmers in Ukraine. The lawyer grew up in Kyiv. What drives her, she says, is her family's fate. That's what keeps her going.

My grandfather, Baldur von Schirach, was the Reich Governor of Vienna at the time. 'Every Jew active in Europe is a danger to European culture,' he said in a speech in 1942. He was responsible for the deportation of Jews from Vienna, and for the fate of the lawyer's family. This was 'a positive contribution to European culture', he said. Perhaps my anger and shame at his words and deeds have also shaped who I am.

I ask her where these crimes originate, why they exist. She looks silently across the table into space. 'Hate is the starting point,' she says after a while. 'Even if the Holocaust and the murders in my country aren't comparable – it's always hate, rooted in stupidity.'

Her mobile rings and she stands up. She has to go, she says, her eyes tired. We say our goodbyes.

I sit back down and order myself another coffee. The weather is mild – a long, late-summer Berlin afternoon. Technicians have begun suspending huge video screens inside the Sony Center. An international blockbuster is premiering tomorrow and Hollywood stars are expected to attend.

The People's Court stood a few metres from here. From 1942, its president was Roland Freisler. He was responsible for more than two and a half thousand death sentences – his trials were state-sanctioned murder. Many of his hearings were filmed. One clip shows Field Marshal von Witzleben, who took part in the 20 July assassination plot. He is emaciated from his time in prison and, because his belt and braces have been confiscated, has to hold on to his trousers to stop them slipping down. Freisler roars at him: 'Why do you keep fiddling with your trousers, you dirty old man?'

On 3 February 1945 snow lay in Berlin, the air was bright and clear. That day, the Allies carried out an air raid. Freisler ran towards the bunker. In the court-yard of the People's Court, he was hit by a piece of shrapnel and died instantly. His briefcase contained papers for the trial of Fabian von Schlabrendorff, a young officer who had tried to assassinate Hitler. Freisler would undoubtedly have sentenced him to death, just like all the others before him.

After the war, von Schlabrendorff was appointed a judge of the Federal Constitutional Court and was involved in a number of key rulings. At the time, the Constitutional Court was developing the concept of human dignity in West German law. That the word *dignity* appears at the beginning of our constitution is not coincidental; its most crucial assertion is that 'human dignity is inviolable'. This first article has an 'eternity guarantee' – it can't be changed as long as the *Grundgesetz*, or Basic Law, is in force. The notion of human dignity was the brainchild of the Enlightenment. It can overcome hatred and stupidity. It is life-enhancing because it recognises our mortality, and only through this recognition do we become human beings in any deep and meaningful sense. But dignity isn't part of a person like an arm or a leg. It is only an idea. It is fragile and we must protect it.

The lawyer from Kyiv was right. According to Berlin's Research and Information Centre on anti-Semitism, 947 anti-Semitic incidents were recorded in the German capital in 2017, 60 per cent more than in the previous year. Hate is the most terrible, most basic and most dangerous mentality in the world. It's getting worse, and these kinds of hate crimes have long since ceased to be an isolated phenomenon. But what can we do?

Erich Kästner wrote: 'The past must speak, and we must listen. Until then, we and it will find no peace.' This is very true. We need to understand how we have become who we are. And what we might once more lose. After all, as our consciousness evolved there was nothing to suggest that we would one day act by principles other than those of our prehistoric ancestors. If things had developed according to the rules of nature, we would merely have used our enhanced abilities to kill those weaker than ourselves. But we did something different. We gave ourselves laws and created ethics that don't favour the strong, but protect the weak instead. This is what makes us human in the highest sense: respect for our fellow human beings. Three thousand years ago, King Cyrus of Persia emancipated Babylon's slaves, declaring for the first time that all people were free to choose their religion, and that they were to be treated equally no matter what their background. Cyrus's laws form the first four articles of the Universal Declaration of Human Rights. If we don't protect minorities today – regardless of whether they are Jews, migrants, asylum seekers, homosexuals or others – then we will fall back into the depths of darkness. The English Magna Carta, the American Bill of Rights, the French Déclaration des Droits de l'Homme et du Citoyen, and the constitutions of today's free world – these are our victories over nature, our victories over ourselves.

Even if we feel the greatest reluctance to address the brutalities that are currently taking place, we have no other choice. Only we are capable of confronting the barbarism, the rage, and outpouring of bile.

I once asked the lawyer from Kyiv why she was shouldering all this herself. 'Who will do it otherwise?' she replied.

19

In 1962, a forty-year-old married woman decides to get sterilised. The doctor who carries out the procedure is convicted. Celle's Higher Regional Court rules the sterilisation to be a form of bodily harm, because the woman had merely wished to pursue her 'uninhibited craving for pleasure'.

In 2017, a woman sues a clinic for compensation. Her husband had undergone several operations on his spine, was now impotent, and her 'previously fulfilling sex life' had been 'adversely affected'. Hamm's Higher Regional Court dismisses the claim.

20

There comes a time when you no longer have any heroes. You know too much. Too much about yourself and too much about others. For me, Michael Haneke is the one exception. Art isn't a democratic process or a social undertaking – quite the opposite. It needs to be uncompromising, and I know of no other artist who compromises less. The precision of his work, the lack of sentimentality, the absence of any clichés – all of this has often sustained me when I've felt like giving up.

Ayumi came from Kyoto to study music at the College of the Arts in Berlin. Almost every day for three years, she played the piano in a tiny practice room. In the summer, she left the window open because it got too muggy. My chambers were near the college, and sometimes, when I passed under her window, I would stop and listen to her for the duration of a cigarette.

From time to time we met up in a café. She liked the pear tart. We talked about her practice sessions, about her teachers and about haiku – short-form Japanese poems. She said they had the same immediacy as music. Anyone could understand them right away. She particularly liked a haiku that the monk Ryokan had dictated to a nun shortly before his death. Ayumi wrote it out in German and Japanese on a paper serviette and read it to me in both languages:

At times showing its back
and at other times its front,
a maple leaf falls.

The fourth or fifth time we met up, something strange happened: she suddenly stopped talking mid-sentence, then gazed out of the window, her body completely still. Only after a few seconds did she carry on, in a way that implied nothing had happened. Over a number of weeks, the pauses became longer, and in the end I asked her what was going on.

'D'you know,' she said, 'I'm falling out of time.' First her language disappeared, then the café, the trees, the pavements, and finally herself. In these moments, she said, it became still, everyday troubles melted away, all the things that were dark and difficult. It was a start, at least. She smiled as she spoke. I thought I understood her. I was wrong.

During her final year concert, she suddenly lost consciousness and slid to the floor, hitting her head on the piano. An ambulance took her to hospital; she was X-rayed and the doctors discovered a brain tumour the size of a table-tennis ball.

Her parents flew over from Japan. Her father was a small man with heavy, horn-rimmed glasses, her mother wore a black dress. They bowed to the doctors and said very little. When I saw Ayumi for the last time, she had lost the ability to speak, her lips were as white as her skin, it looked as though she no longer had a mouth. She died a few days later.

Her parents wanted to bury her at home. I helped them with the paperwork, it was all I could do. We watched the crate being pushed into the hold of the plane. It was an ordinary crate, the kind used to transport surfboards or floor lamps or aluminium struts. But inside the crate was a wooden coffin, and inside the wooden coffin was a zinc casket that had been soldered shut, and within it lay wood shavings and peat and Ayumi in a white dress.

The plane took off like every other plane that day. I sat for a while in the airport lounge and waited for something to happen. People looked at their phones, ordered food and drink, and discussed the football results. That was all. I got a taxi home.

That evening I saw Haneke's film *Caché* for the first time. I'd already been a criminal defence lawyer for over ten years at that point, but it was only there in the cinema that I completely understood the nature of guilt for the first time. Psychologists and psychiatrists tell us there's no such thing as guilt – they think these kinds of statements are helpful, and perhaps they are. But it isn't true. We do things that make us guilty, every single day. In Haneke's *Happy End*, people kill – they hurt, betray and keep secrets. They can't help it. They stand side by side, they don't touch each other, they don't acknowledge each other, they find each other irksome and embarrassing. All of them are lonely and all are strangers to themselves. When they think they've found love, they write about sex and destruction in the blue light of a computer screen. At one point, thirteen-year-old Eve says to her father: 'I know you don't love anyone. You didn't love Mum. You don't love Anaïs, you don't love this Claire, and you don't love me. It's no big deal.'

Every Haneke film I've seen has unsettled me. It took me four attempts to finish *Funny Games*. Never again have I seen such an accurate film about violence. Its depiction of murder isn't some amusing pop event, like in Tarantino's films. Watching *The White Ribbon* was the only time I experienced total silence in a completely packed cinema. Nobody ate popcorn, nobody coughed, nobody said a word. *Amour* reminded me of *Last Stop*, Imre Kertész's diaries. 'And then finally, after three years of senseless, repulsive suffering, I suffocated her,' Georges says of his wife's death in *Happy End*. At the time, it made me think of Socrates: in his last moments, he asked friends to sacrifice a cockerel to the god of health – death is the cure for life.

For me, at any rate, Haneke's films are like haiku. They say exactly what they want to say, nothing else. There are secrets and insinuations, stories that are never quite resolved, but no metaphors, just as there are no metaphors in life. The image a haiku presents is immediate, it is simple and it is whole. At school we learn the opposite: literature, theatre and the fine arts are meaningful when only a few people understand them. Martin Heidegger wrote: 'Being intelligible is suicide for philosophy.' Complex things, we are told, have value. But that's nonsense. In reality, the simplest things are the most difficult. Haneke's films matter because they make us question ourselves. They show us that there are no answers. This is possibly our sole truth. It took me a long time to understand that.

When I was young, it seemed to me that one of the most important questions was: what is 'evil'? I had just qualified as a lawyer, and my first big client was a young woman who had killed her baby. I went to see her in prison. My head was full of the teachings of great philosophers: I had read Plato, Aristotle, Kant, Nietzsche, Rawls and Popper. But now, suddenly, everything was different. The walls of the prison cell were painted a glossy green, which was meant to be calming. The young woman sat at a tiny table. She was crying. She was crying because her child was dead, because she was locked up, and because her boyfriend was gone. And precisely at that moment I understood that I had always asked the wrong questions. It's never actually about theories and systems. Life lasts just a brief moment and in a few years we'll all be dead. We are finite, fragile and vulnerable, and even though we sometimes think we can, we're never able to fully understand our lives. Over two hundred years ago, Goethe wrote: 'People are born into limited circumstances; they are capable of understanding simple, near and definite goals . . . but as soon as they go beyond these limits, they know neither what they want nor what they ought to do.' The validity of this statement lies in its modesty. For me, in any case, concepts like 'evil', 'good', 'morality' and 'truth' have become too vast and too broad. For twenty years, I've defended murderers and killers, I've seen bloodied rooms, chopped-off heads, mutilated genitals and dismembered corpses. I've spoken to people on the edge of the abyss, who were naked, destroyed, bewildered and horrified at themselves. And after all these years I've grasped that the question of whether a person is good or evil is a completely futile one. For people can be anything: they can compose *The Marriage of Figaro*, paint the Sistine Chapel and invent penicillin. Or they can wage wars, rape and kill. It's always the same person, this dazzling, desperate, tormented human being.

'The helpless, complete subjection to an entirely alien and threatening entity: life, nature; to a state of being that is hostile to people, to existence; to a growing darkness, to silence, to madness.' This is what Michael Haneke wrote as a young reviewer about Thomas Bernhard's novel *Extinction*. Today, it seems to me to be a manifesto for his films. Of course, we want an explanation for everything – that's ingrained in us, we can't help it. We're just beginning to understand how life came into being biologically, and we're close to comprehending the origins of the universe. But we won't find an answer to the crucial question, the *why*. After all, we can't rise above our language, we only ever understand our lives using *our* minds, we can only ever describe them using *our* concepts – we don't have anything else. But these concepts mean nothing to nature, to life, to the universe. Gravitational waves are neither good nor evil, photosynthesis doesn't have a conscience, and we can't be for or against gravity. It's all just there. In the end, it's like the famous quotation from Blaise Pascal's *Pensées*, which Thomas

Bernhard used to preface his novel *Gargoyles*: 'The eternal silence of these infinite spaces terrifies me.'

But what does it mean? Is there really no one sitting in judgement over life? And what if there is? Isn't it possible that we're mistaken? We don't know. So we must come to terms with the fact that it's just as foolish to say life has a meaning as it is to say the opposite. Haneke asks us precisely these questions. But this isn't a cold nihilism or cynical worldview, or a turning away or giving up. It's the opposite. We leave the cinema feeling unsettled, we realise that we need to think deeply about ourselves. 'That's the whole story I wanted to tell you,' says Georges to Eve in *Happy End*.

21

I've been invited to give a reading in Jena. That afternoon, my agent sends me a message: my Turkish publisher has been shut down by the president's 'emergency decree'. Now only my play is still being performed in Istanbul and Ankara.

Over 130,000 civil service employees have been dismissed, including 4,000 judges and state prosecutors. More than 77,000 people have been detained. The state has closed down 193 media outlets and publishing houses, and 160 journalists now find themselves in prison. The organisation Reporters Without Borders speaks of 'repression on an unprecedented scale'.

İsmail Kahraman, the president of the Turkish parliament, declares: 'We will break the hands, cut out the tongues and destroy the lives of those who attack our values.'

I go for a stroll in the old town as there's still a bit of time. Dannecker's bronze bust of Schiller stands on a pedestal outside the university's main building. In 1789, Friedrich Schiller gave his inaugural lecture there: 'Ours are all the treasures that diligence and genius, reason and experience, have finally brought home down the ages of the world.'

22

Jordan. We spend four days negotiating in an air-conditioned skyscraper of steel and glass in Amman. In the evening, I look out over the ancient city from the roof terrace of the hotel, the luminous pink of the wide sky. Three thousand years ago, the Greeks called this place *Philadelphia*, 'brotherly love'. A few miles away, people are killing each other. The hotel manager says that four million Syrians have already sought refuge in his country.

After everything is signed, I still have a day before my return flight. I want to see where *Lawrence of Arabia* was shot, so I rent a Land Rover and drive to Wadi Rum. I get out between two granite crags. I take off my jacket and sit down in the shade – the temperature is nudging thirty degrees. Everything here is vast, slow and silent. I leave the camera in the car. The desert can't be photographed, just as the sea can't be photographed, or the sky, or the night. There's no destination here, no past, no story. The desert isn't made for humans, and humans aren't made for it.

On 4 January 1960, Albert Camus is planning to travel to Paris by train. Michel Gallimard, who along with his wife is staying with Camus in Lourmarin, offers to give him a ride. He has a new Facel Vega, a dark green four-seater coupé. Although Camus has already bought his ticket, he accepts the invitation. His children take the train.

The road is narrow and made up almost entirely of bends. The American engine is too powerful for the elegant French chassis, the steering imprecise with too much play. At Villeblevin, at around two o'clock, one of the tyres bursts. The car smashes into a plane tree and breaks in two. Camus is killed instantly. Gallimard dies five days later in hospital. His wife, daughter and the family dog survive.

Later, the police find Camus's briefcase lying by the car. In it are his passport, his diary, a Shakespeare play, Nietzsche's *The Joyous Science* and, most importantly, the manuscript of his new novel. It's called *The First Man*.

This final novel depicts the beginning of his life, his

childhood in the heat of Algeria, the taciturn inhabitants of that world, the poverty. In a note, Camus says he wanted to write the book as a letter to his mother. Only in the last line does the reader discover that she can't read.

It's possible that Camus never wrote anything better than this. His images are hard and spare, sharply delineated shadows. They're like the sand in this desert valley, which cuts into the skin.

23

It's six in the morning and he's sitting on the bed. He smokes a cigarette, even though it's forbidden. The hotel room is just like all the others he's slept in: two bars of chocolate in the brown minibar, shrink-wrapped peanuts, a yellow plastic bottle opener advertising something or other, a chair made of light brown imitation leather. His company booked the hotel. The print-out says 'best price guarantee', a smart card serves as his key and mostly doesn't work. There's 'free Wi-Fi', a 'spacious seating area', and a 'modern sports bar' with 'live coverage' next to the reception desk. The room smells of disinfectant and hotel soap, the floral carpets are designed to absorb every sound.

He's been married for fifteen years. He can't stand her any longer. The way she eats, the way she breathes, the way she moves in her sleep, the colour of her nail varnish. He's never said anything to her, he's not the kind to complain, but the past two years have been unbearable. He has to do it, he'll explain everything to her. After all, I only have one life, he thinks, there's no dress rehearsal and no encore. And then he gets all tangled up in his thoughts, because he doesn't want to hurt her, and because he's lonely and feels stupid and selfish. His father – he often thinks of him these days – was a barber his entire life. When he got old and couldn't cut hair anymore, he still washed the towels and swept up the hair on the floor. This man, who was married to the same woman for over fifty years, never had any doubts. 'A marriage like that does drag on,' he'd said, 'but what can you do?'

There's a glossy magazine on the table, a woman on the cover, a docile face. Those other things no longer exist, he thinks: the battered briefcases, the clocks with their faded dials, even the writing paper and pens have disappeared. His smartphone is 'border-less' – it's like the functional art on the room's walls, the piped music in the lifts and the TV that greets him by name. The fruit on the table has been polished. A cigarette company's brochure lies next to it. They've developed a device that only heats the tobacco rather than burning it.

Suddenly he remembers the woman who happened to sit next to him on a plane a few months ago. As they were landing, she had asked if she could hold his hand. They'd stayed like that in their seats for a long time afterwards. He never saw her again.

He thinks of the countless men who have slept in this room before him. He imagines their lives: a wedding in a hotel like this, with a foyer of imitation marble, glass and brass. Then kids, a new car, a mortgage on a house or an apartment, their hopes pinned on new orders and the annual bonus. Here, they dreamed of the blonde receptionist and wore navy suits whose trousers they ironed in this room on the fold-out ironing board. And then, one day, they sit on the hotel bed as he is doing now. That's how it always ends. The world owes him neither pity nor solace, he knows that.

Four months later, he still hasn't left her. At the weekend, they go to the cinema, a romantic film she's keen to see. He collapses in the central aisle. He lies on the red carpet in the popcorn he's just bought for her. He doesn't like popcorn himself, but now it's sticking to his trousers and his shirt and his hair. At the hospital he has a second heart attack and dies.

24

A prime-time talk show. It's harmless stuff – the politicians get a bit heated at times, the presenter calms them down again.

At the same time, on so-called 'social media', there's a running commentary on the programme. The talk show guests are 'primitives' and 'antisocial psychopaths'; one of the men is an 'ugly bastard', one of the women a 'tax-dodging lesbian'. The others are 'drunkards', 'snitches' and 'lying traitors'. They need to be 'given a good thump' and to 'have their balls cut off'. Theirs are *lebensunwerte Leben* – 'lives unworthy of life' – a loaded National Socialist term.

The late-night news features the leader of a party that holds some seats in the Bundestag. He's shown at a rally, saying: 'Hitler and the Nazis are just a bit of bird crap in more than a thousand years of glorious German history.' This isn't accidental or a slip of the tongue, there's no typo in the script. The politician meant to say what he said: sixty-five million dead soldiers and civilians and six million murdered Jews don't count. He knows his baying audience, he knows what they want to hear, and he knows what journalists will report. It is the kind of language that alters our consciousness.

A few weeks later, federal police officers accompany a Tunisian on a flight from Düsseldorf to Tunis. He is said to have given Salafist hate sermons in mosques and to be a former member of Bin Laden's bodyguard. He's termed a 'dangerous individual', but no law can explain what this actually means. In actual fact, the man has never been convicted – eleven years ago the Federal Prosecutor's Office halted proceedings against him due to a lack of 'suspicious circumstances'. The 'dangerous individual' was not deemed to be 'a suspect'.

Three complaints lodged by this man are subsequently heard by the Administrative Court. The authorities want to deport him. The Administrative Court rules that this won't be possible as long as his hearings are ongoing. The court faxes the ruling to the police, but it arrives too late: the plane has already been airborne for an hour and a half. The Administrative

Court now orders the man to be brought back. His deportation is 'grossly unlawful' and 'violates fundamental principles of the rule of law'. The city takes legal action to try to prevent his return and loses: no authority may ignore ongoing hearings or rulings, and the courts must be able to depend on this being so. The Higher Administrative Court speaks of a 'manifest' violation of the law. The individual who happens to be involved is completely irrelevant – the law protects those who despise it too.

The editor-in-chief of a bourgeois newspaper pens a short piece for the online edition. The court's ruling, he writes, demonstrates that the constitutional state is functioning as it should.

The readers of the article are furious and immediately post hundreds of comments on the newspaper's website. The editor-in-chief is threatened with 'punishment'. 'The Administrative Court's decision is just "technocratic noise",' writes one, while another asks: 'What kind of law, if you please, doesn't help the German people, but harms them instead?'

Hans Frank was one of Hitler's first followers – as early as 1923 he took part in the Munich Beer Hall Putsch.

The Nazis called people like him 'Old Fighters', which was meant as a term of respect. Hans Frank became the Minister of Justice in Bavaria and, shortly afterwards, the 'Reich Commissioner for the Coordination of Justice in the German States and the Restoration of the Legal System'. Later he was Governor-General of Poland, where he was known as the 'Jew butcher of Kraków'. At the 1933 German Jurists' Conference, he declared: 'Everything that benefits the people is just and correct, everything that harms them is unjust and wrong.'

25

It takes nearly four hours. The notary reads slowly, seems to ponder every sentence. The lawyers, who have been negotiating the text for weeks, wear expensive suits and big watches. The subject: factories, shares, land, houses, container ships and a yacht in the Mediterranean. Every detail is being settled – the executors, the administration of the will, inheritance tax. I'm just sitting in, I know nothing about inheritance or tax law. The client has asked me to be there, perhaps because I was once able to help her out years ago. Beneath the window lies the old town – medieval dormer windows, shutters painted blue-white or green, seven hundred years of bourgeois respectability.

Finally, the notary is done. Is everyone in agreement, he asks? The client looks at the lawyers, they all nod. She signs the papers, her handwriting a little shaky. I've never seen her with a mobile phone, impossible to imagine her in front of a computer screen. She is eighty-four years old, weighs maybe fifty kilos and is very ill. After her death, her assets will be transferred to a charitable foundation. That's what she has put in writing here today.

After the signing, everyone stands up and shakes hands. The client looks tired. One of the office staff brings us our coats.

It's extremely cold outside. The client's chauffeur is waiting by the door. In the car, she says: that's done now, what a relief.

We drive through the old town to an almost empty inn. The walls are papered with old photographs of boxers, interspersed with posters advertising big fights. It's a strange spot for this old lady, who doesn't seem to belong here. The innkeeper greets her warmly and leads us to a table. The inn went bust a few years ago, she says. It would have been forced to close, so she bought the building. The innkeeper only has to pay her a very modest rent.

'You know, this inn is the last link to my past,' she says. She goes over to the photos. She refers to the boxers by their first names and has an anecdote about each one. For the first time today I see her smile. I ask her to tell me more.

'You probably won't believe this, but the only man I ever loved was a boxer, a heavyweight. My parents were against the relationship – he's no man for you, they said. Later, of course, I married twice, but it was never the way it was with him. I always parked the big car I drove as a young woman a few streets away so he wouldn't see it. I didn't want him to know my family had money. When he finally found out, he couldn't have cared less. I loved him for that as well. We always met here. It wasn't like today – boxers were social outsiders then, people looked down on them, so they had to stick together. He taught me all about boxing. Everything I know about the world, really,' she says.

A waitress brings us menus with wipeable plastic covers. We order a snack.

'Do you know anything about boxing?' she asks.

I shake my head.

'Boxing,' she says, 'is violence, courage and control. Of course, it's all about winning, about flooring your opponent. But contrary to what most people think, boxing is anything but primitive. It's the opposite. Street fighting is primitive, destroying an opponent with knives and clubs, with kicks and choking and so on. But boxing is utterly inconceivable without civilisation. There are a great many rules. The boxer mustn't hit below the belt, he mustn't strike the opponent with his elbows, shoulders, forearms or the edge of his hand. Headbutting isn't allowed; no punches to the back of the head, to the kidneys, or use of the knees, feet or other parts of the legs. All that's allowed is punching with a closed fist. It's not about the violence itself, it's about the staging of violence.'

When she smiles, she looks like a young girl. I've never seen her like this. Maybe it's because she put her estate in order today, a whole day spent discussing her death and what will follow.

She tells me a bit more about her boyfriend, the boxer. He was an extremely tough man, who really had fought his way up from the humblest of backgrounds. He was strong, a man capable of protecting her, not as refined as the bankers and managers and lawyers she knew from her parents' house. At the time, she couldn't have articulated it, but today she knows that what attracted her was the danger, the violence, the proximity to death, the finality and lack of compromise. 'Back then we were immortal,' she says. With him she felt safe.

What became of him, I ask?

She gazes into space and doesn't respond; her lips are thin and pale again. Then she shows me his photo on the wall above the counter, a tall man with a square chin, his hair combed back with pomade. I try to imagine what the old lady looked like sixty years ago. Next to him she must have seemed like a child.

Later, her chauffeur drives us back to my hotel. As I start to get out, she puts a hand on my arm and leans forward. 'He died from a wasp sting at a picnic. Anaphylactic shock, heart attack,' she says. 'I've never been able to forgive him for that.'

26

A reading in Munich, then to Upper Bavaria by car, a few days in an idyllic landscape. A hundred years ago, Wassily Kandinsky, Franz Marc, Paul Klee and Lovis Corinth painted this blue land with its soft light. Ödön von Horváth built a summer house in Murnau in the 1920s, Bertolt Brecht bought a house on the Ammersee in 1932, and Thomas Mann's *Doctor Faustus* is set in a village nearby.

I'm invited to visit Benediktbeuern Abbey, with its mighty copper beech in the courtyard garden. The abbey church: playful Italianate baroque that takes a childlike joy in excess. In the sanctuary above the altar hangs a huge golden clock. 'With hasty step death comes to man, it grants him not a moment's stay.' When Schiller wrote these lines in *Wilhelm Tell* he was forty-six years old – he died just a year later. In the abbey shop next to the church, one of the fathers shows me spiritual and self-help books, tea lights and embroidered sayings. People can't manage more than that these days, he says.

I make my way through the villages of Lake Constance to Freiburg for a reading. Memories everywhere. I spend the night in Lindau, in a hotel opposite the medieval Mangturm and the six-metre stone lion in mid-roar. The most beautiful house on the lakeside promenade is the tax office. Far off, high above the lake, the snowy Alps gleam.

The following day I drive past orchards and vineyards, a serene, happy landscape. But unlike in my childhood, the villages and towns are overrun now. A stop in Nußdorf, lunch with friends, then a solo trip to the lido. Admission costs three euros. There's no one lying on the grass, it's still too cold to swim. I sit on the bench under the old willow tree whose branches hang down in the water. The lake is perfectly smooth. This is where I first read Thomas Mann's *Magic Mountain* one summer forty years ago. Back then, I didn't understand a word of it, because I didn't yet know what *time* was.

Later, rapeseed fields and farmers' meadows, gentle, pale green hills, then down into the Black

Forest, named for its gloom by the Celts. Charcoal burners and glass blowers lived here; everything was dirt, poverty and misery. Today, tourists in colourful functional clothing with shiny hiking poles wander around the place. Only those familiar with the winter nights can see the reality, the darkness.

Then Freiburg. The cathedral dominating the heart of the city, the heart of thought. The minster tower, elegant in its severe simplicity. After my reading in the theatre, a stroll back to the hotel. The fifteenth-century houses with their thick walls and tiny windows – constraint that gave protection. Erasmus lived here for a few years. If he, the quiet and cautious one, had prevailed instead of the noisy Luther – the moderate instead of the revolutionary – what would the world have become? Today there are pretty restaurants and shops in the old houses around the minster. I visit a café with a sign stuck to the door: 'self-service'. The customers have little backpacks, there are laptops and iPads lying around on the tables, many of the young men sport beards on their childishly soft faces.

As a boy, I often visited the theatre here – my boarding school was only sixty kilometres away. One of the older priests usually accompanied us on the coach. He told us that Lessing's *Nathan the Wise* was the first play to be performed in that theatre following the war. He loved the play and would explain it to us over and over again. The priest taught Greek and Latin. No one had ever seen him get angry. He never raised his voice. He had served as a soldier in the past: he and his brother, a Munich lawyer, had been part of the resistance against Hitler. It was only later, a few years after the war, that he joined the Jesuit order.

The boarding school owned a hut up in the mountains. It had an open fireplace, and we were sometimes allowed to spend the night there at weekends. We were eight boys, all between ten and eleven years old.

On that particular day, the day I'm recalling now, it had snowed the whole night. The morning was very cold and very clear. The deer lay behind the woodpile. It was still alive, its left front leg caught in the iron trap, the bone fractured, it had lost a lot of blood. We had found the trap in the shed. We had opened it up and sprinkled sunflower seeds and oat flakes on the ground before it. We had imagined catching a wolf or a bear, even though there were no wolves or bears around. Now the deer lay there, scared and bleeding to death in the snow.

The priest knelt down by the deer. He put his hand over the animal's eyes, stroked it and then broke its neck. It was quick. He fetched pickaxes and shovels from the shed, and we dug all morning. The ground was frozen solid. We placed the deer in the hole; blood got on the priest's soutane. He didn't call the animal a 'creature of God', he didn't erect a cross and he didn't say a prayer. The snow was dirty now, and we felt tired and ashamed.

The priest said that a man needs just three qualities: he must be bold, brave and gentle. He should start things boldly, bear their failure bravely, and treat people gently. He died when I was twelve, and was laid out in the private chapel of the boarding school. His face was bluish-white and for the first time since I knew him, he wore a soutane that wasn't covered with bits of ash and food. I liked the old man.

In Greece, the inscription above the entrance to the Temple of Delphi read: 'Know thyself'. The god Apollo gave this advice to the Greeks, the old priest wrote it up on the board in our first lesson, and today the phrase is printed on T-shirts and bumper stickers. But it's impossible. No one can know themselves. We know of death, and that's it, that's our whole story.

27

There's a staff discount for food in the hospital canteen. At the till, a man asks for the discount. The cashier hasn't seen him here before. He's a doctor, he says, but doesn't have his ID on him. The sum in question is 1.95 euros. The man is well-groomed, he wears a suit and tie. He claims he's giving a lecture to the urologists at the hospital. He's from Munich, he adds, because she just looks at him without saying anything.

There's a psychiatric department at the hospital. The cashier knows how to tell the crazies. It's their gaze, their inability to hold eye contact, and the way they smell — furry, musty, like spoiled mushrooms. The cashier leans forward and sees that the man is wearing slippers. It's now that she finally refuses him the discount.

After her shift, she sees the man's face on a screen in the hospital foyer. At home, she looks him up on the internet. His Wikipedia entry says he always wears slippers because he suspects a link between tight shoes and kidney disease.

And now she's sure that she wasn't mistaken.

28

I made Kramer's acquaintance for the first time after he'd sold his company. The buyers had accused him of falsifying the accounts, which led to a protracted trial. The files were made up of thousands of pages, spreadsheets, tables and expert opinions. Countless papers had to be read out in court; we negotiated every other day for eight weeks. At a certain point, purely out of exhaustion, everyone was ready to compromise and we reached an agreement.

The evening the trial finished, there were no more trains to Berlin. I was tired and would gladly have stayed put in my hotel room, but Kramer invited me to dinner. The hospitality of strangers is some-times the worst kind. I said I would join him later.

According to the papers gathered by the court, Kramer had been convicted numerous times in his youth. Theft, robbery, extortion and assault. At the age of nineteen, he'd received a heavy juvenile sentence. He had started a fight with two bouncers because they wouldn't let him into the village disco. Both were over six feet tall and martial arts experts. Kramer didn't stand a chance. With a broken rib, smashed jaw and gashed face, he dragged himself to his car. There he waited for four hours, in what must have been excruciating pain. When one of the bouncers entered the car park, Kramer started the car, ran him over, shifted into reverse and ran him over again. The bouncer died on the way to hospital.

Later, in the juvenile detention centre, a social worker assessed Kramer as being 'intelligent, aggressive and incapable of empathy'.

At around ten o'clock, I went to the Ratskeller. It was supposed to be the best restaurant in town – a dark interior with oak floorboards, wooden tables and rich food. Kramer had brought along his girlfriend, the company accountant and the latter's wife.

The accountant's wife was beautiful. She was wearing a black sheath dress and high heels, and carrying an expensive French handbag. She didn't seem to fit with the accountant and she didn't seem to fit with the Ratskeller. She looked like she was finding the whole situation awkward.

When I got there, Kramer had already drunk too much and his speech was slurred. When he saw me, he yelled for the waiter. 'Bring champagne,' he shouted, before turning to me. 'About time. We need to celebrate the end of the trial.'

The waiter brought over a bottle and some glasses. Kramer crumpled up a banknote, stuffed it into the waiter's shirt pocket and whacked him on the chest with the flat of his hand. 'Good man,' he said. He took the bottle, shook it and popped the cork against the ceiling. Some of the other customers turned to look. Champagne foam splashed onto his girlfriend's blouse. 'Wipe that off,' he said, and tossed a napkin across the table. He poured the drinks, spilling half in the process. Then he sat down again. His face was red and he was breathing heavily.

'Just before you arrived,' he said, 'I was telling the others about something I read in the paper today: half of all married men are unfaithful.' He paused. A vein in his left eye had burst. 'But if that's so, then half of all women must be unfaithful too. It doesn't add up otherwise, does it?' He laughed.

Kramer's accountant had been the key witness at the trial. He had an impressive memory, knew every figure off by heart. He was a nondescript man, who wasn't particularly well paid and had a slight stutter. No one in court doubted his honesty. It was largely thanks to him that Kramer had avoided conviction.

Kramer stood up, leaned over the table and clapped the accountant on the shoulders with his small, fat hands. He always brought his head too close to people when he spoke to them. He had bad teeth and bad breath. The accountant tried to smile.

'Can you imagine? Half of all wives screw around.' Kramer addressed his staff with the informal 'you' as a point of principle. 'One in two wives,' he shouted. 'Even your lovely wife could be at it. She's too good-looking for you in any case.'

The accountant didn't reply.

'Don't look so dumb,' Kramer said, and sat down again. He yelled for the waiter and ordered another bottle.

Kramer's girlfriend, a young woman with chubby cheeks, put her hand on his forearm. 'Leave them be,' she said gently.

Kramer pushed her hand away and stood up again. He took off his jacket and tie. His shirt was soaked with sweat around the collar and under the braces at the back. He drew a roll of banknotes, secured with a thick, red rubber band, from his trouser pocket. 'So here's what we're going to do. This is five thousand euros. I bet you that one of the two women at this table is cheating on us.' Kramer threw the roll of cash into the middle of the table.

I said that I was very tired and it would be best if we all went home now – it had been a long day. Kramer's girlfriend nodded and began to get up. Kramer, who was still standing, pushed her back down by the shoulder. 'You stay right where you are.'

'But even if that were true, Mr Kramer,' said the accountant calmly, 'you could never prove that a woman was being unfaithful.'

'Actually, it's really easy. Her mobile. You just need to look at the last few text messages. That's exactly what it said in the paper.'

Kramer had put his girlfriend's handbag on the table and was rummaging through it. 'Where's your phone?' he asked.

Because he couldn't find it straight away, he tipped the contents of the bag onto the table. He picked up the mobile, which was lying among the lipstick, glasses case, sweets, pills and tissues, and tapped in the code, which he clearly knew. After a few seconds he said, 'There you go – nothing. Just texts to me and her mother.'

Kramer turned to the accountant's wife.

'Where's your phone?'

'I don't have it on me,' she said.

'Rubbish,' slurred Kramer. 'Everyone has their phone on them.'

'I really don't.'

Kramer stared at her without moving. Thin strings of spittle had formed between his upper and lower lip. Finally, the woman put her handbag on her lap and undid the clasp. Kramer spotted the mobile, reached into the bag and pulled it out. He held the phone up in the air.

'Well, well, look what we have here,' he said. 'And the code?'

'I . . .' said the woman.

'Ah yes, of course we've forgotten the code too. Should have known.' He paused for a second. 'The code. Come on.' His voice sounded sober again, it was clear and sharp. Now I understood what his employees had meant when they called Kramer 'intimidating' during the trial. Most of them were afraid of him. One said on the witness stand that they had dubbed him 'the slave driver'.

The accountant's wife gave him the number in a quiet voice. Her lips were pale.

'That's enough now,' I said, and stood up.

Kramer wasn't listening anymore. He stared at the phone display for a long time. Then he switched it off and gave it back to the accountant's wife. It was quite dim in the restaurant, but I think I saw Kramer bow slightly to her. Then he sank back into his chair.

'You win,' he said to the accountant. His voice now had a different, weary tone. He seemed exhausted.

'But I didn't accept your bet,' said the accountant. That was a mistake.

'Take the money, you idiot.' Kramer gave the roll of banknotes a shove. 'Go on, dammit.'

The accountant hesitated for a moment, then pocketed the cash.

I'd had enough and said my goodbyes.

'Do you want a lift to the hotel?' asked Kramer. He pointed at his girlfriend. 'She's driving.'

'No, thanks,' I said. 'It's not far, I'll walk.'

As I was paying my hotel bill the following day, I saw Kramer standing in the lobby. He was freshly shaven and in good spirits.

'I wanted to say goodbye,' he said. 'And, well, to apologise for yesterday. I simply had too much to drink. Do you have a minute?'

I ordered a taxi and we sat down in the lobby.

'You know, when I got out of prison at the age of twenty-four, I had a girlfriend,' Kramer said. 'We married, she got pregnant and we had a baby boy. She always had this way of saying *Come over here*. That's all she needed to say, I still remember it to this day. I had to promise I wouldn't go breaking the law again, otherwise she wouldn't have taken me on. At the time, I worked as a painter in the construction industry – I'd done my apprenticeship in prison. Everything went well. For a while, anyhow.'

Kramer lowered his eyes.

'Four years later, I beat up a man with an iron bar on a building site because he'd given me some lip. My wife left me; she'd warned me that she would. She said it was so hard loving me and she just couldn't do it anymore. She moved to the north of Germany with our son. It took me fifteen years to get over it. In that time I built up the company I've just sold.'

Back then, he said, he'd started eating too much and piling on weight – the travelling, hotels and conferences hadn't helped either. He kept on eating because he'd felt nothing mattered anymore. The only relationships he had were with prostitutes. To be honest, he despised people who looked like he did now; people who had given up on themselves. He was going to stop overeating and get his body back into shape. That and everything else.

'What are you going to do?' I asked.

'I don't know. I've made more money than I can spend. Perhaps I'll visit my ex and finally see my son. I think I could do that now.'

The concierge came over to let me know my taxi had arrived. We got up and Kramer walked me to the door.

'Don't you want to know what was in the woman's texts?' he asked.

'I don't think so,' I said, and climbed into the taxi.

He lived in a life nothing happened at many. The only thing was the pull of his seasickness. Only hunger, he despised himself who looked like he did nothing but eat and eat and drink and smoke. His was a way to stop on time and gorge, both black livers and liver. That and everything else.

"I'm pressed," Jerry Curtis hinted.

"I told him I've made every penny that I can spend. I told you," he said. "And really, I'm sure and I think I could do this now."

"The easiest thing now is to let the smoke air fade in and smoke. We both would've never pulled me to the bed.

"Oh, I'm your work now. Where's she in his wagon?" Jerry he said.

"I don't think so," I said, and pushed him into the car.

29

The Coen brothers' film *The Man Who Wasn't There* depicts the humdrum life of a smalltown barber. His wife starts an affair with the owner of the local department store, complications arise, things get out of hand, and eventually the barber kills the department store owner. He and his wife are charged with murder.

They hire a money-grabbing, big-city lawyer. He stays at the swankiest hotel and dines daily on lobster spaghetti. One scene shows him standing in the prison while the accused couple sit on wooden chairs and a private detective leafs irritably through his notes. The film is shot in black and white; the visuals are stark. In the course of his visit, the lawyer comes up with the defence strategy for the trial. He says:

'They got this guy in Germany. Fritz something or other. Or is it . . . Maybe it's Werner. Anyway. He's got this theory. You wanna test something, you know, scientifically – how the planets go round the sun, what sunspots are made of, why the water comes out of the tap . . . Well, you gotta look at it. But sometimes, you look at it and your looking changes it. You can't know the reality of what happened or what would have happened if you hadn't stuck in your own goddamned schnoz. So, there is no *what happened*. Looking at something changes it. They call it the uncertainty principle. Sure, it sounds screwy, but even Einstein says the guy's onto something. Science, perception, reality – doubt. Reasonable doubt. I'm sayin' sometimes the more you look, the less you really know. It's a fact. A proven fact. In a way, it's the only fact there is. This heini even wrote it out in numbers.'

In 1801, Kleist wrote to his fiancée: 'We are unable to determine whether what we call the truth is truly the truth or whether it only seems so to us.' Kleist wasn't doing very well at the time. Success had eluded him: his plays had been censored or banned outright. Up until the end, his family – almost all of whom were in the military – failed to understand him. In a number of his letters, he explains his condition: it's an all-encompassing feeling of alienation. According to many of his biographers, Kleist became depressed after reading Kant's *Critique of the Power of Judgement*, but I don't buy that: people don't despair because of books. It's the other way round. We seek out the books that are written for us. In Kleist's case, it was Kant who explained to him why the ground had fallen out from under his feet – in other words, what we call reality.

A hundred and twenty-five years after Kleist, Werner Heisenberg explains: 'The reality we can put into words is never reality per se.' He says it is impossible to simultaneously measure two properties belonging to one particle exactly. If you determine the precise location of a particle, this invariably changes its energy.

We live for just a blink of an eye, then we vanish again, and in this brief time we're not even capable of seemingly the simplest thing: knowing what is real.

To this day, no one has disproved Heisenberg's theory.

30

It's crowded in the dining car of the train – just one free seat available, opposite a woman. I ask if it would be OK to sit there and she nods. She's wearing black sunglasses that are too large for her face. It takes me a moment to place her: we first met thirty years ago – she was the daughter of a well-known academic and an ambitious young woman. Even as a schoolgirl, she had helped stick up election posters. Later she studied political science and joined a centrist party. I saw her a few times on talk shows; she was starting to build a solid career as a local politician. Now she seems old, stiff and drained of energy. We talk about the weather, about the train delays and dreadful food.

Suddenly she asks: had I not heard about what happened 'back then'? She's amazed I don't know. She'd said this one sentence in the state parliament. Twenty-five years she'd been in politics – she'd never harmed anyone, always been courteous, never made personal attacks on her opponents, not even in the heat of election campaigns. She'd wanted to perform her duties to the best of her ability. Her specialist areas had been the economy and culture, and she'd known her stuff pretty well. And then she had said this one sentence in parliament.

What she experienced afterwards was almost indescribable. At first, journalists had written 'unfathomable' things about her. Then things had kicked off in the internet forums and on social media. Being called a 'filthy pig' was relatively harmless, but then she'd been threatened with rape, torture and murder, told she was human scum. She'd been sent emails containing sentences that even now she couldn't bring herself to repeat.

For weeks, she could only sleep one or two hours a night. It was simply relentless, she was battered day in day out. She lost fifteen kilos in weight. She wasn't a religious person, she'd had a progressive upbringing, but in the end she felt like she'd committed a terrible sin and was being punished by a higher power.

After six months, she finally cracked. She broke down in floods of tears on the pavement outside a department store. Her husband had to admit her to a clinic. Psychotropic drugs, followed by two years of therapy.

Only the fact that her children still needed her had stopped her from ending it all. She'd been forced to give up politics entirely, even though it had been her calling, a fundamental part of her life since her youth. Today she worked in the state library's administrative team without any contact with the public – that simply wasn't possible anymore. She was still afraid of other people's rage.

What was it she had said, I ask? She lowers her voice still further: '*Even paedophiles should be given a chance to rehabilitate.*' She stirs her cold tea with a spoon and looks out of the window. Beyond it lies the landscape of Fontane, flat, barren and grey.

In 1955, Emmett Till, a boy from Chicago, was sent down South by his mother for the summer vacation. He was to stay with relatives in Leflore County. Emmett was a teenager. He told the rural boys about his big-city adventures with women. They called him a bragger. If he was genuinely that experienced, he'd have to prove it by approaching the good-looking lady in the small local store.

Emmett got up his courage, went into the store and exchanged a few words with her. He didn't know the rules – Emmett was Black, the woman was white, a former beauty queen.

Several nights later, the woman's husband and his brother drove to the house where Emmett was staying. They abducted the boy. His body was found three days later. The perpetrators had beaten him half to death, then shot him and thrown him in the river with a weight around his neck. Emmett Till was just fourteen years old when he died.

That same year, the two men were put on trial. The jury deliberated for only an hour before the judge announced the verdict: acquittal.

Three months later, the two men were interviewed by a magazine. They said they had found a photo of a white girl in the boy's wallet, which sent them into 'raging fury', and that was another reason why they had killed him.

The two men were never punished. The law protected them from fresh criminal proceedings in spite of their confession.

On the train platform in Hamburg, I say goodbye to the woman. Her husband is there to meet her, an older gentleman. As they are carried up by the escalator, he puts his arm around her shoulders. Their raincoats are the same colour, they blur into one another.

31

In a terror attack in Brussels, two bombs explode at the airport and another in a metro station. Thirty-five people are killed and over three hundred injured.

That evening, the German Minister of the Interior looks into the cameras and says: 'Data protection is all very well, but in times of crisis like these, security takes priority.'

32

The Russian anaesthetist assures him that she knows what she's doing. She's in something of a hurry – the words *emergency surgery* quicken every movement here. She seems very young. She's been a consultant for five years, she says, and has considerable experience. The problem is always the same: people think she's too young when she's wearing this gear. She pulls off the green surgical cap, wants him to see that she's actually older. She doesn't realise she looks even younger that way. She smiles, or at least he thinks she does.

She carries on talking in her harsh Eastern European accent, but he's no longer listening. The only word he retains is *propofol*. He imagines how long a journey she's had from a suburb of Minsk to the hospital in Berlin, how proud her parents must be, how many sacrifices there were, how many lucky breaks.

The operating theatres are down in the basement. There's more space there, a senior doctor once told him. Wire cages filled with laundry, neon lighting, empty beds with plastic covers, a surreal place like a cliché from a bad film. He tries to say something, but can't anymore. The blood runs freely from his back, saturating the sheet, dripping off the trolley onto the corridor floor. The doctors are animated, sterile packs are being ripped open, quiet orders given to the theatre nurses. A cleaning lady will mop up the blood later, he still has time to think.

It's only bewildering to begin with; the last moments are completely free of fear. Things become bright, then translucent, then airy, and then still. Life leaves his body, lessens with every beat of his pulse, happening of its own accord, without effort, without anguish. Any preparation for death while we're still alive is pointless, he knows that now. He thinks one more time of the woman he loves. She had glowed, he had always seen her like that, a warm glow, like the old lamps upstairs in the old house of his youth. *I'm watching over you*, that's what she had told him every night before he went to sleep. Then this thought fades too, it has nothing to do with him anymore. The end is but a gliding: gentle, painless and without any noise. Everything about it is right, death is the best invention of life.

Four days later, he's allowed to visit the little park in front of the hospital for the first time. A young couple are asleep on the grass – he has his arm around her, his head is bandaged. A taxi driver is cleaning the windows of his car. Cyclists, mothers with children, women wearing hijabs, a man with a fat belly. You can buy ice cream from a securely moored boat. He counts the swans on the water, watches the patients feed them with dry bread from the hospital. Then his phone rings and life goes on.

33

Every morning, I pass the old drunk. He sits on the bench that the supermarket installed. When he drinks, he holds the schnapps bottle with both hands. Before him, a paper cup with a few coins. It's *his* bench. I've never seen anyone else sitting there.

Last night, the drunk was still there, but he was no longer moving. His head was tipped back, his mouth wide open, his breathing laboured. His skin was yellow, presumably some kind of alcohol poisoning. I walked past him at first, then turned back and asked if I could help in some way. He slowly came to, saliva running from his mouth and dripping onto his shirt. He looked at me and shook his head. 'I have no skin,' he said.

This morning his bench is empty.

34

The late-night news shows images of a volcanic eruption in Guatemala – sixty-two dead, thousands of local residents forced to flee. The volcano has raged for two days. Bodies lie under smoking piles of rock, houses are caked in mud up to their rooftops. A geoscientist explains what caused the catastrophe. Then footage of an open-air Christian mass, people praying to God in a meadow. The priest speaks of *el mal*, evil, and of *el malo*, the devil.

Evil exists, but how did it come into the world? Every great theologian and philosopher has grappled with this question. God is all-good and all-powerful. But if He created evil, He cannot be all-good. And if He did not create evil, but was unable to prevent it, then He is not all-powerful.

Even so, believers don't doubt. They say that evil doesn't come from God, but from people instead. Or that it's simply a void, like a hole in the ground, and not something that was created at all. Or that evil is precisely a sign of God's goodness. Or that we're simply not in a position to understand why it exists. In any case, they'll keep believing in goodness and redemption, in their God, who no longer demands blood sacrifices.

A young woman sits on a camp bed in a tent, her face swollen, she's crying. Her three-year-old daughter was hit and killed by a lump of rock, she says into the camera.

35

I'm meeting with an art historian. In 1938, according to a newspaper report, the Nazis looted a Viennese family's belongings. My great-grandfather then 'bought' one of the paintings from their collection.

After the war, the Allies seized my great-grandfather's and grandfather's assets. Just a few years later, my grandmother was allowed to buy the painting back from the Munich authorities. She paid hardly anything for it. In a matter of days, so the newspaper says, she had sold it for a substantial profit.

The descendants of the Viennese family now live in New York. The painting was never returned to them.

The art historian will advise on the options open to me now. After being a defence lawyer in numerous criminal cases, I know that explanations can sometimes help the victims. Only by understanding evil can we continue to live with it.

In the taxi, I look again at the photo of the stolen painting in the newspaper. It's pretty – a peaceful square in Holland, a red-roofed house with a sign hanging from it, a cathedral with two towers in the background; men, women, children, trees, a blue-grey sky. The picture is probably only a copy, the article says – it's practically worthless. But that isn't true.

Georg was a childhood friend of mine. To begin with, our parents weren't allowed to visit us at boarding school, and we could only go home during the holidays and call our parents once a week. It wasn't until the third year – when we were thirteen years old – that the Jesuit priests relaxed the rules. I don't know whether it was because we were older or because they realised that this sort of thing didn't fit the times anymore, but from then on we were allowed to go away every third weekend.

Georg lived just eighty kilometres from the boarding school, so I would often spend the weekends at his home. He lived on Lake Constance in a small eighteenth-century castle. His parents were plump, with red faces that looked like the summer apples from their garden.

On those Sundays, at the insistence of Georg's parents, we always had to visit his grandmother as well. She lived in two low rooms under the eaves of the roof. The old lady hadn't left her bed in a long time.

Each time, Georg and I would put off this visit until shortly before our departure. The heating in her room was turned up high; even in summer, it was dreadfully hot. The old woman's voice, her eyes and her smell were unpleasant. Whenever we were up there, we were made to stand side by side before her bed. She would ask us about school, about our grades and our teachers, and if we answered correctly – we almost always lied – she gave us each a coin, which she extracted with thin fingers from her black purse.

There were countless paintings in Georg's house: dark still lifes with pheasants and partridges, ancestors wearing suits of armour or velvet dresses, and copperplate prints of hunting and riding scenes. Only the old lady's room contained a painting that didn't go with the house or its inhabitants. She had hung it opposite her bed: a South Sea scene, two naked women lying on a beach, a yellow dog playing between them. Vibrant colours, expansive brushstrokes, figures without shadows. I always wanted to take a closer look at it, but didn't dare in front of the old lady.

Many years later I visited Georg at his home in Hamburg. We were adults ourselves now and Georg's children were at university. He had married into a wealthy family and made a fortune in property. The house he lived in had been built in the 1920s and was decorated as such houses always are: Bauhaus lamps, Eames and Jacobsen furniture, ornamental bookshelves and green sofas. There was lots of comfortable seating on the terrace, from where one had a view over the river Elbe.

Above the fireplace hung the painting from the room in which his grandmother had spent her final days. Georg said it was a fake, a miserable copy of a Gauguin. He had read his grandmother's diaries, which were found in her bedside table after her death. Unbeknown to her relatives, she had spent a few years in Madrid after the war. Presumably, she had gone there to escape the scrutiny of her family.

She'd had a lover in Madrid, a painter. And this man had given her the painting. Georg's grandmother, who had always seemed to us to be a dull, stern old lady, wrote in her diary: 'He is the only man with whom I am *complete*. Dying is not so terrible, but ceasing to love is. Now, for the rest of my days, half is all I shall be.' She quoted a sonnet by Michelangelo: 'Nel vostro fiato son le mie parole' – 'In your breath my words are formed.' She was twenty-three at the time. Three years later she married Georg's grandfather and moved with him to the little castle on Lake Constance.

We stood in front of her South Sea painting for a long while. And then Georg said that this worthless painting was the most important thing he owned.

In Berlin, the art historian explains the current situation to me over lunch. The legal position in relation to stolen artworks is complex. He describes international conferences, administrative bodies and foundations, and talks of the difficulties of conducting any kind of research. Even the benchmarks in this field are yet to be fully established, he says.

I think of the South Sea painter and of Georg's grandmother, and that our memories are all we are. The past is never dead, William Faulkner once wrote. It's not even past.

36

A married couple – he a construction driver, she a housewife – have been together for nearly forty years. Their children have long since left home. After his retirement, he gradually becomes a burden. He drinks heavily night after night and hardly ever bothers to shave. She has to beg him to shower at least once a week. When he talks, she feels like he's droning on, and she can't bear to look at him anymore. 'What else is there to look forward to?' he keeps asking.

For her, it's the opposite. Now that she no longer has to take care of a household with four children, she goes to the theatre, readings and concerts. She reads newspapers online, meets up with old friends and does lots of walking. She lays out new flower beds in the front garden of their terraced house.

One morning, at the height of summer, she wakes early. He's lying next to her, snoring. He smells of alcohol and garlic; the hair on his back is slick with sweat. She rests her head on her hand and studies him. Suddenly, she knows what she needs to do. The idea seems so pure and so clear, so unshakeably true, that she actually feels physically rejuvenated. She gets up, makes herself a cup of tea and sits on the steps of the house with a book. It's the first day she's felt happy again in a very long time.

Over the next few weeks, she experiments with a caoutchouc-based toothpaste. She found the recipe on the internet, but it doesn't work right away, even though she's often made teas, salves and oil infusions from plants in the past. When, after a number of tries, the mixture actually looks like toothpaste, and no longer tastes awful thanks to some mint, she adds in the coniine. She had grown the hemlock in her little front garden.

She fills a jar with the paste and puts it in the fridge. And then she waits. It takes nearly six months. Finally, as so often before, he gets toothache. He has chronic tooth decay because he's always been scared of going to the dentist. She's so sorry, she tells him, there aren't any painkillers in the house, she forgot to buy more. In actual fact, she has disposed of all the pills.

She's loving and caring, she strokes his back. Maybe there *is* a way she can help him, she says. She's made a highly effective plant preparation that would give him quick relief. She fetches the toothpaste and not only gets him to brush his teeth with it, but to hold it in his mouth for five minutes and then swallow it. She knows how difficult this must be, she says, it burns like hell, but he's her big, strong man, isn't he? She knows he wants to look brave in front of her and she gives him a smile. It'll get better in a minute, she says as she stands in the doorway of the bathroom. She hasn't smiled at him like that in ages.

The neurotoxin causes paralysis to rise from the feet into the spinal cord. The victim suffocates while fully conscious. She's read up on all of this. When the death throes begin, her husband starts flailing about, beside himself with panic and pain. She pulls the bathroom door shut from the outside and locks it; she has moved the key round in advance. When she hears him fall to the floor, she dons her gardening apron, goes into the front garden and carefully rakes the flower beds. Two hours later she unlocks the bathroom door and calls the emergency services. Later, the police find two of the man's teeth in the shower tray; he had broken them off as he bit down on its edge.

After a trial by jury, she is sentenced to seven years' imprisonment: she had admitted everything straight away in her first police interview. It's a lenient sentence and the judges go to great lengths to explain why this isn't murder, but an exceptional case instead. She is a delicate-looking woman with a soft voice; her hair is neatly styled and she wears a simple black dress. Seated at the defendant's bench, she folds her hands and lowers her eyes, but when she's addressed, she raises her head, answers clearly, and looks at the judges with an open gaze. She describes her marriage and her husband's decline – she barely has to lie. Only one of the police detectives, a witness at the trial, says that she is an emotionally cold woman, calculating and selfish.

She's a model prisoner. The social workers like her, her cell is always clean and tidy, she enjoys taking part in group sessions with the psychologist. She's released after four years. Even on her final day, she makes her bed in the morning, she can't help it. While in prison, she sold the house that she'd shared with her husband. The only thing she'll miss is the garden, she tells the prison chaplain.

Following her release, she moves into an airy, two-room apartment in the city centre. Ten months later, her probation officer writes a report for the public prosecutor's office: she has settled in 'brilliantly', meets up with girlfriends, takes courses at the adult education college. Her children also pay regular visits.

In her final hearing before the sentencing board, she says that she's happy now and that it would never cross her mind to commit another crime. She has a new life partner. The judges remit the remainder of her sentence. She is fifty-six years old. And she is free.

Sometimes she tries to remember how things were. She knows that she loved her husband once, right at the beginning. 'To everything there is a season,' she murmurs, looking at her new boyfriend. He's four years younger than her and extremely well-groomed – 'clean', she thinks. They plan to marry and move to a house in the suburbs. It has a small garden.

37

Jean Fouquet's 'Melun Diptych' is on display at the Gemäldegalerie. Usually, only the left-hand portion of the painting hangs in Berlin – two men gazing into space. The Madonna on the right-hand side is absent: it has hung since the nineteenth century in Antwerp's Royal Museum of Fine Arts.

Today I see the painting of the Madonna for the first time. It looks oddly plastic and anatomically incorrect; the red and blue of the seraphim and cherubim are luminous, trying to evoke a 'celestial' mood. Agnès Sorel, a young woman from the ranks of the minor aristocracy, was the model for the painting. The front of her dress is unbuttoned, her left breast is bared, but she isn't nursing the Christ Child sitting on her lap.

Agnès Sorel was considered the most beautiful woman of her time. She is said to have introduced the 'fashion of the exposed breast' to court, with dresses whose low-cut décolleté allowed ladies' breasts to be seen by all. She was mistress to the French king and later became his advisor. He made her rich, gave her a swathe of castles and appointed members of her family to prestigious posts.

A few metres further on is Caravaggio's *Cupid as Victor*, a naked boy with grubby toes, laughing cheekily as he sits on a globe of the world. The painting's original title, 'Amor Vincit Omnia,' comes from Virgil's *Eclogues*: 'Love conquers all; so let us too yield to love.' Caravaggio doesn't distinguish between the sacred and the profane – for him there is only life itself.

When Agnès Sorel, the beautiful Madonna, died, her last words were said to be: 'How disgusting, fetid and fragile we really are.'

38

It is the biggest table I've ever seen, cut from a single tree trunk. I don't understand how they could have got it up to the twenty-second floor of the skyscraper. Its surface is completely smooth – it looks like a Jeff Koons artwork. About thirty bankers and lawyers are ranged on either side of the table, women and men clad in identical sombre colours. In front of each there's a laptop.

When the president of the bank enters the room, everyone briefly rises to their feet. With a wave of his hand he bids us to be seated, and takes his place at the head of the table. He is very tall and very thin. All he has before him is a notebook. His hands are covered with age spots, his neck is lined, his face deeply tanned. He wears his watch over the cuff of his shirtsleeve, which would look ridiculous on anyone else, but on him looks pleasingly eccentric. The president is well over eighty and inherited the bank. His family is said to have financed the Suez Canal and the plunder of the Congo by Belgium's King Leopold II. Some even claim that the bank covertly 'made' three American presidents. He is one of the richest men in the world. He owns mines, freshwater springs, tech companies, automotive suppliers and even the rights to a rock band's catalogue.

You can't hear the air conditioning, but the room is ice cold. I've been invited to say a few words about corporate criminal liability in Germany, but no one asks me any questions.

A young man positions himself by the huge screen on the wall. He presents blue, yellow and green bar graphs, pie charts and diagrams in rapid succession. He speaks quickly, his pupils dilated, he's perspiring. The subject is a bug in the software that slowed thousands of transactions by milliseconds. Some of the bank's clients lost a lot of money. When the young man is done, he immediately leaves the room — presumably to take some more cocaine.

A lawyer summarises the investors' lawsuit against the bank. She explains where she sees openings for the defence and says that the court will dismiss the case. Following her presentation, everyone looks at the president. He asks who the judge is and receives a name. The president nods, everyone seems relieved. The president expresses his thanks, gets up and exits the room.

In the corridor afterwards, I have a quick chat with two lawyers. There's a video installation on the wall next to us. The images are disconcerting: they show red ants running across the open eyes of various faces. Then an assistant in a suit and high heels escorts me downstairs.

I meet the president's son for lunch in a London club. I first met him fifteen years ago at a dinner in Marrakesh, where he was living under an assumed name and was keen to be an artist. His paintings were a bit dull, rather decorative and pretty, but he had talent. Later, he invested in a start-up that was developing a fitness watch, sold the company to a sports goods manufacturer for a large sum of money, and was subsequently of the view that he had worked enough for one lifetime.

While we're eating, I remark that his father is an agreeable old gentleman. The son starts laughing so loudly that other diners turn around. 'No, no,' he says. 'He's literally anything but that.'

Eight years earlier, he had turned up unannounced at his father's place in the country – typically for him, he'd forgotten to call ahead. As ever, instead of using the main entrance, he had cut through the garden and walked up the outer flight of steps instead. The French doors were open, which meant that he could see his father and his wife without them realising. What I should also know, he adds, is that she was his father's sixth wife, an underwear model. She was only twenty-two when they married; his father had been seventy-one at the time. 'A love match, of course – what else,' says his son.

The young woman was kneeling naked on the wooden floor, her lips painted red and her hands tied behind her back with a horse's bridle. His father was sitting on the sofa in light blue silk pyjamas, throwing cherries at regular intervals from a paper bag onto the floor. The young woman had to gather them up using just her mouth and then spit the stones into a small silver bowl. With each new cherry stone, his father, this elegant, highly respected man with aqua-blue eyes, the president and owner of a four-hundred-year-old bank, this world-renowned patron and philan-thropist, said to her: 'Very good, my little Maggie Thatcher, very good.'

39

A friend has died, ridiculously early, at the age of just fifty-eight. His wife and two children are standing by the open grave.

When I was sixteen, following my father's death, my uncle gave me a slim book: Epictetus's *Enchiridion*, a handbook of morals. Epictetus was a lame slave. He had been bought by one of Emperor Nero's advisors – all rich citizens had an educated slave at the time. His master allowed him to study and gave him his freedom after Nero died.

When philosophers were banished from Rome, he was forced to flee as well. He moved to a small Greek island. For the whole of his life, he owned nothing more than a lamp, a sack of straw, a bench and a blanket made of rushes. He died at the age of eighty in around AD 130. He himself never wrote anything – his books were composed by his pupils.

My uncle had served in the navy during the war. A shell tore off his left arm and three fingers of his right hand. After the war, he studied law and became a judge, ultimately presiding over jury trials.

The copy of *Enchiridion* he gave me was the one he had carried in his coat pocket during the war, which then lay on his bedside table in the military hospital and later on the judge's bench.

It opens with these lines:

Some things are within our power, others are not. Within our power are: receiving and comprehending, motivation, desire and refusal – everything that we ourselves set in motion and are responsible for. Not within our power are: our bodies, our possessions, our social standing, our status – in short, everything we have not set in motion ourselves and are not responsible for.

These sentences sound simple, but at the time I didn't understood them. Epictetus didn't create any brilliant philosophical systems. His handbook of morals really contains nothing but daily exercises, and its consolations are simple, human and clear. He shows what we can change, what we must accept, and how to distinguish one from the other. That is all.

When you kiss your child or your wife, say to yourself, 'It is a mortal that I kiss.' Then you will not lose your composure when they die.

One of my dead friend's children is four years old, a handsome boy with blond curls. His mother tells me that he laid his stuffed toy giraffe in his father's coffin, so that he wouldn't be so alone there.

You can live by Epictetus's words as long as nothing is happening.

40

More than twenty years after we both qualified, I meet Baumann by chance in court. I almost don't recognise him as he's lost about fifteen kilos. We used to call him 'Schubert', because his full lips, curly hair and round glasses made him look like the composer. Now he's a gaunt man with hardly any hair and a very pale complexion. We arrange to meet for dinner.

His chambers are in Kreuzberg. They consist of three rooms and a mature lady with a Berlin accent who takes care of his admin. The rooms look like a lawyer's office from the 1920s: high walls, stucco, wood panelling, metal lamps, a wooden table topped with green linoleum in the meeting room. The walls are bare, no pictures, and case files are neatly stacked in open wooden cabinets.

Baumann tells me that his clients are people from the neighbourhood. He deals with legal disputes that arise between traders at the market, with wills and marriage contracts. 'Bread-and-butter stuff, very little out of the ordinary,' he says. 'Now and then I take on small defence cases, always trifles: car accidents, bar fights, libel and so on.'

None of this seems to fit. He passed his exams with distinction, then studied for a year at Columbia University in New York. He was awarded his dissertation *summa cum laude* – a very complex piece on Roman law. After qualifying, he took a job with a high starting salary at one of the big American law firms that had settled in Berlin after the fall of the Wall.

When we were junior lawyers, he struck me as a bit odd. He believed with great seriousness in notions such as guilt, atonement and forgiveness. 'The law can reform people,' he said, and really seemed to mean it. Baumann was very shy back then. If a woman so much as came near him, he would go quiet, blush and look down at his feet.

The four tall windows of his office look out over Chamissoplatz: apartment buildings from the late imperial era, renovated stucco facades, cobblestones, street lamps. Officers once lived here, then factory workers, says Baumann, and now the flats are often rented by artists.

We walk to a nearby Italian restaurant. He dines here every evening, always at the same time. The waitress tries to flirt with Baumann, she calls him 'Dottore'. He doesn't reciprocate. We tell each other anecdotes from when we were trainees.

Later, he invites me to his apartment, which is above his chambers. It's as stark and austere as his office. In the living room there's just a sofa, television and bookshelf. Baumann isn't married – he has no girlfriend, no children, no siblings, his parents are both dead. I ask him what he does to keep himself busy. During the day he's downstairs in the office, he says, the evenings he spends by himself. He has no hobbies. 'I watch the news, read a little and then I go to bed.'

Baumann makes me a coffee and pours himself a whisky, then he opens the door to the balcony and we take a seat outside. He smokes a cigar. 'These are my vices,' he says.

'Are you happy?' I ask him.

'Content,' he says, and shrugs his shoulders. On this summer evening, people are sitting out on the benches around the square – mothers with prams, a group of older men with a crate of beer. A boy is practising how to juggle – he isn't that good yet. We watch him.

'Your life has turned out differently to how I imagined back then,' I say.

'Yes, perhaps. Our actions have consequences,' he says. 'When you're very young, you don't know that. You only find out later on.'

He takes a drag on his cigar. The smoke disperses above us in the warm air. And then he tells me his story.

Baumann was thirty-three years old. He specialised in insolvency law and had already had some success. Two months earlier, he'd been made a junior partner at the firm. He worked hard and everyone thought he had a brilliant career ahead of him. Many of his colleagues considered him to be arrogant, but actually he was just reserved.

Baumann was working on a complicated settlement when the receptionist called to tell him that he had an unexpected visitor. A bit annoyed at the interruption, he left his office and took the lift to the ground floor. When he entered the meeting room, he found a woman standing with her back to the bookshelf. They shook hands. She said that criminal charges had been brought against her. She needed his help; he'd been recommended by friends.

Up until then, Baumann's relationships with women had been fleeting and few. Now, as he attempted a smile, he noticed that he was blushing and his hands were damp. The woman looked like a model from the 1960s – a boyish body, dark eyes, black hair, a slender neck that was almost white. All of a sudden, Baumann felt dirty. He remembered how he used to watch the girls getting changed at the swimming pool when he was a boy. His cases typically involved the seizure of assets, insolvency estates, inventories and segregation issues. His only knowledge of criminal cases was from his time as a trainee. He stared at the woman's mouth and from that moment on he was lost. Barely listening to what she was saying anymore, he had her sign two powers of attorney that granted him the authority to act for her, and made a note of her address. When he got up to see her out, he knocked over the bottle of water on the table. He apologised and gave a sheepish smile.

That afternoon, Baumann applied for permission

to see the case files, and two days later had them brought to him by courier. The case sounded simple, just as most criminal cases do at the start: a wealthy married man had begun an affair that lasted a few months, then his wife had found out. The man was forced to break up with the mistress in order to save his marriage. On the day the relationship ended, the sum of 100,000 Deutschmarks was transferred from his account to his mistress's account, something that was also 'discovered' by the wife.

Up until that point, the facts of the matter were plain, but then the statements diverged. The man claimed that his mistress – Baumann's new client – had stolen the money, transferring it herself without his knowledge. She had done so on his laptop, which had been lying around open. Baumann's client said that was a lie. The man had given her the money as a parting gift to salve his guilty conscience.

There was no evidence to support the man's accusation – apart from his own statement. The transfer had been made on his laptop, but of course no one could say who had authorised it. Granted, the sum involved wasn't a small one, even for a wealthy man, but the client had never committed an offence. She had no criminal record and lived in 'respectable, middle-class circumstances', as a police officer noted in the case file.

The public prosecutor's office had the woman's apartment searched and her mobile phone examined. They found bank documents, payment reminders, letters and photos – nothing unusual. The police printed out almost three hundred pages of text messages stored on her mobile. They, too, provided proof of the love affair but not of the criminal charges.

Baumann read through the case file and the evidence folders in his chambers. He worked as diligently as he did on insolvency proceedings, compiling lists, extracts and notes from the files. After a few hours, he found what he was looking for. Entry Number 27 in the police evidence log was a 'notebook'. It had been filed away in a plastic sleeve in one of the folders – a small, light green, leatherbound book. Thus far, the police hadn't copied it for the case file, probably because the investigators had deemed it irrelevant. His client had filled the first thirty pages with shopping and to-do lists that had no connection to the alleged crime.

But Baumann was thorough: he read the notebook page by page. Halfway through, it unexpectedly turned into a diary, with notes on the past few months.

In it, the client described the entire affair in a series of bullet points. Baumann looked up the date of the break-up. The diary was clear: out of anger, a sense of grievance and revenge, she had transferred the money from his account to her own while he was taking a shower in the hotel room. 'He has to pay,' the client had written.

Baumann drove home, made himself a strong coffee and began to read through the folder containing the lovers' text messages. To begin with, they were cautious, tentative, polite. He was charming, she was flattered, each was intrigued by the other. Gradually they became more open, then more intimate. Baumann immersed himself in the dialogue between the lovers. There was never a word out of place, every sentence sounded heartfelt. After four hours, Baumann felt like he knew his client inside out. He knew how she reacted to her lover's questions, what she liked, what made her uncomfortable. He saw her wounds, the softness and the sadness within. She stood before him, naked and alive. I have all that in me too, he thought.

At around five o'clock he went to bed. A few minutes later he got up again. He took another look at the photos. In one picture, the client was sitting on the passenger side of an open-top cabriolet. She was wearing a light-coloured dress, large black sunglasses and a straw hat. Baumann took the photo to bed with him and fell asleep with it in his hand.

Two days later he rang the client. He wanted to discuss the case with her, he said. For an hour – far too comprehensively, given the simple facts of the matter – he explained the evidence. He read her the man's statement, he showed her the bank documents and the folder with the print-outs of the text messages. Then he laid the diary before her on the conference table. These entries, he said as emphatically as possible, would convict her in a court of law. There was unfortunately no reasonable defence that could end in an acquittal.

Baumann knew exactly what he was doing. He had thought through every word, every gesture. He looked at his client and waited until he was sure she had understood.

He left the meeting room for ten minutes, saying that he needed to wash his hands. In the toilet he could feel his pulse beating in his throat, he was shaking. When he came back, the diary was no longer on the table. They exchanged a few more words, trivialities he later couldn't recall, then got up to say their goodbyes. She leaned over the table and kissed him on the cheek. 'Thank you so much,' she said softly. Her perfume smelled of iris, jasmine and vanilla; it was a promise. He could see the outline of her small breasts under her blouse.

Four weeks later, the public prosecutor's office dropped the case. There was lack of sufficient proof, the ruling said: aside from the man's testimony there was no evidence of the client's guilt.

Baumann asked the client to meet him again in his chambers. By now, he was feeling excited. In the meeting room, he read her the ruling from the public prosecutor's office. Perhaps I sound a bit too upbeat, he thought. When he had finished, she nodded. She was wearing a tailored dark blue dress with a white hem and a pair of dark blue shoes. He thought of the photos – he knew what she looked like naked.

Baumann believed his new life was beginning at that exact moment. Perhaps she would surprise him by suggesting a trip? Over the past few weeks, lying awake at night, he had repeatedly imagined how they would travel together to the cities he had read about in her diary and text messages – to Rome, Florence, Nice, London. He had enough money saved, he could take care of her, protect her.

They stood up. Baumann took a quick step towards her, pulled her to him and kissed her on the mouth. It was the first time in his life that he had been so daring.

'Are you crazy?' she said, and shoved him on the chest with both hands. He lost his balance and fell back into the chair. She looked down at him from above. For a moment nothing happened: they didn't move, they didn't breathe. And then she laughed in his face.

'You're a pig, just like him,' she said.

That was the last time Baumann saw her. He was never investigated about the missing diary. It remained unclear whether the notebook had been lost at the police station or in the evidence room at the court. These things happen sometimes. Anyhow, since none of the investigators had read it, everyone assumed it was unimportant.

After a long pause, Baumann says: 'She was right.' And after another pause: 'These days I'd rather just look on.'

We sit there for a while in silence. Eventually, Baumann makes his apologies. He isn't used to having visitors and always goes to bed at ten. I put my empty cup in the kitchen and we say our farewells.

Down on the street, I turn and look back up at his apartment. The balcony door is shut and the lights are off.

41

Two old men are sitting at a neighbouring table in the café. As their hearing isn't too good, they talk very loudly.

'It's really hot today.'

'That's because of the weather.'

'Did you hear they shot a doctor?'

'Where?'

'Right here.'

'Oh.'

'He was more in than out.'

'Who?'

'The murderer.'

'In where?'

'The padded cell. He was a brick short of a load. Can't think why they let him out.'

Pause.

'You been to America recently?'

'No, I'd rather not.'

'My mother lives in Canada.'

Pause.

'She's dead now.'

'Who?'

'My mother. I never went to Canada – never got my ducks in a row.'

'I don't go away anymore, either.'

'They're shooting the Blacks there now.'

'It's not like it used to be.'

'True.'

Long pause.

'Or here, either.'

'What?'

'It's no better here, either.'

'But we're in Berlin.'

'It's still no better, though.'

'Was the guy who killed the doctor Black?'

42

'Glittering Seventy-Fifth Birthday Celebration for Town's Most Successful Son,' the local paper will later say. The entrepreneur is the district's biggest taxpayer. Thirty years ago he started a chain of fast-food restaurants. Today, they're to be found in almost every town in the region.

The entrepreneur thanks the mayor and the secretary of state, who has journeyed 'especially' from the state capital to be here. He shakes hands, kisses cheeks, smiles at the photographers, cracks jokes. His assistant whispers the names of the guests in his ear. He can no longer remember most of them.

Over a decade ago, he was held in custody for a few days – a tax offence. After a week in a prison cell, he began reading a volume of Goethe's poems bound in brown paper. At the time he'd wanted to stop, to call a halt to everything, to start a new life. The English word *listen* has the same letters as the word *silent*, he told me in the prison meeting room.

Even in prison, he always carried a faded Polaroid in his jacket pocket. The people in this photograph were his parents, an uncle and himself as a boy, he said. The photo had been taken on his twelfth birthday at a hotel where his uncle was staying. He and his parents had taken the U-Bahn to the city centre. His mother wore a pale dress and a necklace of colourful jewels, his father a tie. He had felt proud. They'd all looked really good that day.

When they reached the hotel, they couldn't find the dining room at first. A waiter wearing black tails and an earnest expression had bowed and led them to a table. He had never seen a waiter like that before, nor rooms with such high ceilings. The table was laid with a white cloth on which stood silver coffee pots and bowls and trays – even the cutlery was heavy. There were cake stands with *petits fours*, black-and-white *mousse au chocolat*, peeled oranges and kiwis, dark honey, yoghurt, sliced cucumber, salmon and horseradish sauce. The uncle, who –

unlike his parents – was very wealthy, had given the waiter a sign, and then a chocolate cake with twelve sparklers was brought out to him. Some of the guests in the room even applauded and congratulated him. A waiter had rolled a small trolley with an ice bucket and a bottle of champagne up to the table. This waiter, who was wearing an immaculate white shirt with a black bow tie and black cufflinks, wrapped its golden neck with a napkin, removed the wire cage over the cork, and soundlessly opened the bottle. He himself had been allowed to take a tiny sip. The glass had been wafer-thin with a decorative gold rim. His father had asked the waiter to take a photo with the Polaroid camera. He had stayed seated, the adults had positioned themselves behind his chair.

Now, of course, it was almost impossible to make out the colours in the photo, he said, but the light in the room had been truly golden. His mother had laid her hand on his forehead; he was quite feverish, she'd said. On the way home, he had kept repeating that he wanted to own a hotel, and that nothing and nobody could ever talk him out of his dream.

That time in prison, the entrepreneur told me he profoundly disliked his fast-food restaurants. The smell of the deep-fat fryers, the smooth laminate flooring, the imitation-wood tables screwed to the floor – all of this had disgusted him for years. The only thing he actually wanted now was softly lit rooms, and there had to be white tablecloths, silver cutlery, champagne and exotic fruit, just like back then. His guests should be the kind of people he enjoyed hosting, people who deserved it. He vowed that he would buy a grand old hotel as soon as he got out of prison. He had decided to transform his life completely, even though it would shock his whole family. He was determined to go ahead. Here, in the prison cell, all had become clear. At last, he said, he was going to do the right thing for himself.

The party is held in the ballroom of the town hall. The entrepreneur's grandson stands close to him, holding on to his grandfather's trouser legs. A waiter brings over a piece of layered cream cake, and he takes the plate even though sugar doesn't really agree with him. He has a lover who is thirty years his junior, they've been together for fifteen years. When he sleeps with her, he's afraid of smelling like an old man. His lover isn't at the party because his wife wouldn't stand for it.

Suddenly he drops the plate, and cream splatters onto his shiny black shoes. He shrugs off his jacket, which slides from his shoulders down onto the floor. The room falls silent. His grandson gets frightened and starts to cry.

The entrepreneur walks swiftly into an adjoining room. He leaves the door open, everyone's eyes follow him. Once inside, he pulls off his shirt and gives a load groan. The hairs on his chest and back are white. He's thin now; he lost twenty kilos during the chemotherapy.

His daughter picks up his jacket and runs after him into the room, closing the door behind her. The guests slowly start talking again and somebody puts on some music – a recording of Schubert's 'Trout' Quintet.

I go out to the car park to smoke a cigarette. Half an hour later, the entrepreneur appears. He's holding his shirt closed with one hand, his daughter has his jacket over her arm, her son is tugging at her dress. The entrepreneur makes his way over to the car, his driver holds the door open for him. He pauses for a moment as he goes by and quietly says: 'I've been cheated. This damned life, it all went too fast.'

43

You need a talent for parties. I don't have it. I always feel like Nick Carraway in *The Great Gatsby*:

> As soon as I arrived I made an attempt to find my host, but the two or three people of whom I asked his whereabouts stared at me in such an amazed way, and denied so vehemently any knowledge of his movements, that I slunk off in the direction of the cocktail table — the only place in the garden where a single man could linger without looking purposeless and alone.

At a certain point, you do meet a person you know, but then some kind of confusion always arises. For a few years now, men have taken to greeting each other with a hug, during which it's customary to bestow several mutual slaps on the back. Everyone shouts at everyone else because the music's really loud. Words don't make sense and you get embarrassed because a woman says, 'Heavens, it must be years,' and all you hear is, 'I've got dirty ears.' While you're still pondering this, a photographer appears with lots of cameras slung around his neck and fires off some flash photos. Then you're blinded for a few seconds and spill your drink and the woman with the dirty ears has gone again. Perhaps she actually said, 'I'd like a beer,' or, 'I must disappear,' or, 'Good to see you here.' The whole thing's bewildering, but in the meantime none of it matters anymore. It gets even louder and even more crowded, a famous singer tearfully recites a line from a washing powder commercial, two young women are wearing exactly the same dress, and a man says he's just ridden naked with Putin through Mongolia.

Much later, I think again of Gatsby's lover and about how her world was filled with orchids – filled with orchestras that set the rhythm of the year, and captured all the sadness and richness of life in new melodies.

44

A dinner after a theatre premiere in London. I'm sitting next to a young opera singer. A few weeks ago she made her first big appearance at the Royal Opera House in Covent Garden, England's foremost opera stage. She sang the role of Donna Anna in Mozart's *Don Giovanni*, a demanding part. The audience and the critics loved her.

Fifteen years of training, she says. A total slog, performing out in the sticks and at little festivals, and then finally, after a hundred tiny steps, Covent Garden, the start of her international career.

She's from a suburb of London. Her father's a bus driver, her mother helps out at a newsagent. It was pure chance that the choir director at her state school discovered her, she says.

Two weeks before her debut, she called her father

and asked him to be there. He enquired what day the performance was. She said: 'On Friday.' He replied: 'Saturday would be better, it's easier to get parking then'.

45

My client's wife calls me to say her husband is dying. I'm to visit him one last time, there's still something he really wants me to tell me.

I don't like travelling by plane – too many people, too many smells. After three hours, the city appears beneath our wings, the sea to the right. The Argonauts lost a boat here during a storm, the ninth of ten ships. Hercules located the wreckage on the coast and founded a city: 'Barca Nona', the ninth ship, Barcelona.

The client's house lies above the city. A guard in uniform yells my name into a radio, then the taxi drives up a long avenue of old cypress trees to the front steps of the house. The client's wife greets me in the entrance hall, her hands are cold. She leads me to the room where her husband is dying. He lies in semi-darkness in his bed, his face sunken, his stubble white. The medical equipment was removed this morning, his wife says, it can't keep him alive any longer.

Many years ago, I had defended this man in court. Back then he was full of energy. He had founded a construction company, and later invested in a company that was working on digitising the human brain and uploading it to a computer. 'That way we can live forever,' he had said at the time. Now he's not even aware of my presence. His wife says he refused further treatment because it couldn't save him and would just prolong his suffering. He's been unconscious since this morning and the doctors say he'll die in the next few hours. She's really sorry that I've come all this way. Unfortunately, she doesn't know why he wanted to see me.

Lots of people are gathered in the big salon downstairs. There are cups of coffee and burnt marzipan pastries. I recognise the firm's in-house lawyer, a tough, elegant woman. I ask her about the software company the client had invested in. She laughs. 'That thing about eternal life? No, it didn't work out. Computer people today believe in technology the way we used to believe in God. They're waiting for the Coming of Artificial Intelligence. It'll have mercy on our souls and deliver us from human imperfection. In Silicon Valley, advocates of new technologies are called 'evangelists', she says. 'Did you know he had his DNA frozen?'

When we're born, an arrow is shot at us that reaches us at the moment of our death. On the flight back to Berlin, shortly before I fall asleep, I think of Marcus Aurelius's *Meditations*. He wrote that Alexander the Great and his mule driver both went the same way in the end.

46

Down at the café, they've set up tables and chairs outside. The owner of the hair salon on my street sits herself down at my table. She's noticed something strange, and now she needs to tell me about it. Every day, a gentleman stops in front of her salon window. He's in his mid-seventies maybe, well-turned-out: jacket and coat, a black walking stick with a silver knob. He always arrives at around one o'clock and then looks in the window for half an hour. It's been going on for weeks now.

At some point she'd asked him if she could help in any way. He'd been polite: no, no, he'd said, he just liked watching her wash her customers' hair. His exact words had been: 'The way you touch all those hairs is so lovely.' The phrase had struck her as peculiar: *all those hairs*. She wasn't sure if this man was dangerous. He didn't look dangerous, not at all, he was an elegant older gentleman, but even so, she was wondering whether she should call the police. He'd been there again today, watching her through the window and giving her a little nod. 'I mean, it's not normal,' she says. Then she talks some more, and each topic gets roughly forty seconds: new hair dyes, asylum policy, a film that's on at the cinema, her daughter's studies, whether Greece should leave the European Union. I fold up my newspaper and pay for my coffee.

In 1886, the psychiatrist Richard von Krafft-Ebing described an odd case. On the first and second nights following a young couple's wedding, the husband contented himself with kissing his wife and 'rummaging through' her hair. Then he fell asleep. On the third night, he asked his wife to put on a long wig. 'No sooner had she done so, than he abundantly made up for his neglected conjugal duties,' writes the psychiatrist. From that point onwards, the husband always brought along a wig, which he first stroked, then put on his wife. As soon as the wife took it off 'she lost any allure for her husband'. The wigs were only 'effective' for ten to twelve days, after which time they were replaced. They always had to have 'lavish quantities of hair'.

The first five years of marriage produced two children and a collection of seventy-two wigs.

47

An 'extreme artist', as he's termed, incubates a dozen chicken eggs in Paris. He sits in a Plexiglas case until the chicks hatch, which takes between twenty-one and twenty-six days. Museum visitors can watch him while he's at it – even the President of the Republic has dropped by. This is his first artwork with living creatures, says the so-called extreme artist. He announces to the media that more will follow.

48

The purchase agreement states:

The contractual item is a classic car. At the time of supply, the sale item was a manufactured product with an anticipated lifespan of ten to fifteen years. On the date of this Contract, the sale item is forty-six years old and has thus substantially exceeded the manufacturer's intended lifespan.

Everyone advises him against buying the old car. It's true, people today are into mobile phones, artificial intelligence and renewable energy. The next few years will see the advent of the self-driving car: it will have an electric or hydrogen drive system and make steering wheels obsolete. It'll also be less dangerous than cars driven by humans. By then, a classic car will seem like a nineteenth-century horse-drawn carriage in the traffic of the 1920s – a completely useless antique.

The car he buys is a Mercedes-Benz 'Dash 8', named after its first year of production, 1968. It looks like a child's drawing of a car or a hat. Paul Bracq, a young Frenchman and possibly the most gifted car designer of his time, came up with it in the mid-1960s. It broke with all earlier forms – no cosiness, no baroque flourishes, no sitting-room-on-wheels. It was a middle-class car: comfortable, but boxy and businesslike, with minimal standard features. Bigger engines and any extras were pricey, but customers could already get hold of headrests, seat belts, electric windows, 'heat-insulating colour glazing' and air conditioning.

The model was a huge success – almost two million were produced. Students ended up driving the now-older cars: the technology and engine were indestructible. The last of the second-hand ones were exported to Africa, where they still often served as taxis. They were simple to repair and even tolerated the heat and dust of the desert.

The car had belonged to an elderly lady from Los Angeles in California. According to the logbook, this lady, who was still a young woman at the time, had got the car directly from the Mercedes factory in 1972. The first service had already been carried out prior to her taking ownership. To begin with, she drove the car all around Europe, and then had it loaded onto a ship and taken home.

No one would bother restoring such a totally average, boring and worthless car, they tell him at the garage workshop. The car has no resale value, every penny spent on it would be a loss. If he wants a classic car, he should go for a fancier model. A 'Gullwing' would be the best choice, or at the very least a 'Pagoda'. But he doesn't want those. No, he says to the garage owner, he happens to like things that have substantially exceeded their intended lifespans. That no one still appreciates this car is exactly what draws him to it. Besides, he doesn't want to sell it on – it's going to be his last car, and he wants to drive it for as long as he can. The owner thinks he's mad, but agrees to do the job.

Six months later, he flies to southern Germany to pick up the car. The departures hall in Berlin is narrow and overcrowded – he's forced to stand. A man is cleaning between his teeth with a bit of paper, a woman wears a red backpack inscribed with the word *Greenland*. He's repeatedly jostled.

He's planning a really long trip. He wants to drive through the old, tired Europe he's believed in for so long and that is currently breaking apart. On the plane, he reads about Louis Vuitton's first successful product. Today, the company prints its oversized logos on shoes, sunglasses and perfumes, but at the beginning of the last century it made only suitcases. In 1904, it designed a model named 'L'Idéal'. It was a wardrobe trunk with small drawers and compartments, and supposedly held a week's worth of clothing: a coat, two suits, shirts, shoes, underwear, socks. A traveller would have need of nothing more, the manufacturer assured people at the time.

After landing, he hails a taxi. The taxi driver takes him to the restorer's workshop. She tells him she comes from Slovenia, from Ljubljana. She misses the cafés there, the orchards in the heart of the city, the river and the beautiful bridges. Ljubljana, which she constantly pronounces *Yubel*, is very different to how one might imagine, a very modern, progressive city. She's really just in limbo here, but soon she'll be able to go back to her city and her family. She keeps talking, a soothing sing-song, and he nods off. He thinks of the 'L'Idéal' trunk and its contents – he doesn't have much more with him now. Nevertheless, he hopes it will be the longest trip of his life. Of course it's all nonsense, he thinks: the old car, his modest luggage, the big trip, his longing for Europe.

Do not go gentle into that good night.
Rage, rage against the dying of the light.

The Ljubljana taxi driver wakes him up when they arrive. The owner of the garage greets him warmly, the restored car is handed over and everything is explained to him in detail. Then he starts the engine and drives off the forecourt. He takes country roads, avoiding motorways. Soon he sees luminous fields of maize, clover, and rape, and masses of yellow gorse. Twice, brown-grey partridges rise from a field. For a moment, he thinks it's a sign.

The car is lovely to drive. He tries to recall the times in his life when he was happy. Perhaps as a child, at daybreak in the bed of the old house, the door to the hallway open a crack. Half asleep, he'd hear familiar morning sounds, voices he knew. Someone was tidying, something was being carried through the house, windows and doors were being opened and closed, dishes clattered, in the hall downstairs his father was scolding the dogs. He had always waited, without quite knowing what he was waiting for. He's sure that he's wasted his life, but doesn't see what he could have done any differently.

On 23 February 1942, maids find the bodies of Stefan Zweig and his wife Lotte in the couple's bedroom. He is lying on his back, his hands folded on his chest. Lotte is nestled against his shoulder, her left hand clasping his right. Zweig had taken an overdose of barbiturates first, then Lotte had waited for him to die before doing the same herself. He left a farewell note: 'Greetings to all of my friends! May they still see the dawn after this long night! I, all too impatient, go before them.'

At the time, Stefan Zweig's books had sold millions of copies. He was wealthy, had a British passport and was safe. Many other German exiles didn't understand his suicide, just as they didn't understand his political restraint. A week after Zweig's death, Thomas Mann wrote in his diary that he found the suicide 'foolish, weak and shameful'.

Thomas Mann was mistaken, he thinks. No one wants to see the dangers others are facing if one has already overcome them oneself. On a sundial in Palermo he had once read: '*Vulnerant omnes ultima necat*' – 'All hours wound, the last one kills'. It makes no difference when that hour is. There is no obligation to live, everyone fails in their own way.

When he gets tired from all the driving, he parks the car by a café in a small town. It has been a horrendously hot day, and he's glad of the air conditioning in the car. It's cooler now, the afternoon sun bathes the town in a liquid amber light. He sits outside the café, it's pleasant here on the shady pavement. Laurels in green tubs, polished windowpanes, a chemist's with an old-fashioned sign hanging outside. A dog dozes by the fountain in the middle of the street – a red tongue, a white belly on the cobblestones.

A couple stands in front of a shop window. As they begin to move off, the young woman places a hand on her boyfriend's arm to make him wait, then kneels down and ties his shoelace.

Happiness is a colour and is always fleeting.

A Note on the Text

These pieces first appeared in the following publications, and were revised for this volume.

'Three': *Rolling Stone*, 29 March 2018.

'Four': *Frankfurter Allgemeine Zeitung*, 17 November 2009.

'Fourteen': *Bild*, special issue, 7 June 2018.

'Sixteen': *Der Spiegel*, special issue on Helmut Schmidt, 2015.

'Eighteen': *Literarische Welt*, 19 May 2018.

'Twenty': Foreword to Michael Haneke, *Happy End: Das Drehbuch* (Paul Zsolnay Verlag, 2017).